Strike While the Duke is Hot

Dukes in Danger
Book 2

Emily E K Murdoch

ARE YOU SIGNED UP FOR DRAGONBLADE'S BLOG?

You'll get the latest news and information on exclusive giveaways, exclusive excerpts, coming releases, sales, free books, cover reveals and more.

Check out our complete list of authors, too!

No spam, no junk. That's a promise!

Sign Up Here

www.dragonbladepublishing.com

Dearest Reader;

Thank you for your support of a small press. At Dragonblade Publishing, we strive to bring you the highest quality Historical Romance from some of the best authors in the business. Without your support, there is no 'us', so we sincerely hope you adore these stories and find some new favorite authors along the way.

Happy Reading!

CEO, Dragonblade Publishing

Additional Dragonblade books by Author Emily E K Murdoch

Dukes in Danger Series
Don't Judge a Duke by His Cover (Book 1)
Strike While the Duke is Hot (Book 2)

Twelve Days of Christmas
Twelve Drummers Drumming
Eleven Pipers Piping
Ten Lords a Leaping
Nine Ladies Dancing
Eight Maids a Milking
Seven Swans a Swimming
Six Geese a Laying
Five Gold Rings
Four Calling Birds
Three French Hens
Two Turtle Doves
A Partridge in a Pear Tree

The De Petras Saga
The Misplaced Husband (Book 1)
The Impoverished Dowry (Book 2)
The Contrary Debutante (Book 3)
The Determined Mistress (Book 4)
The Convenient Engagement (Book 5)

The Governess Bureau Series
A Governess of Great Talents (Book 1)
A Governess of Discretion (Book 2)
A Governess of Many Languages (Book 3)

A Governess of Prodigious Skill (Book 4)
A Governess of Unusual Experience (Book 5)
A Governess of Wise Years (Book 6)
A Governess of No Fear (Novella)

Never The Bride Series
Always the Bridesmaid (Book 1)
Always the Chaperone (Book 2)
Always the Courtesan (Book 3)
Always the Best Friend (Book 4)
Always the Wallflower (Book 5)
Always the Bluestocking (Book 6)
Always the Rival (Book 7)
Always the Matchmaker (Book 8)
Always the Widow (Book 9)
Always the Rebel (Book 10)
Always the Mistress (Book 11)
Always the Second Choice (Book 12)
Always the Mistletoe (Novella)
Always the Reverend (Novella)

The Lyon's Den Series
Always the Lyon Tamer

Pirates of Britannia Series
Always the High Seas

De Wolfe Pack: The Series
Whirlwind with a Wolfe

CHAPTER ONE

March 31, 1810

Henry Everleigh, Duke of Dulverton, almost slipped in something he sincerely hoped was mud.

"Damn and—"

"Bless you, Your Grace," said his manservant severely.

In the early morning light, Henry looked up with a glare. *Why did Jenks say such a ridiculous...*

His thought faded as his gaze shifted from his servant, a little bedraggled after the hours spent in his carriage, to the gaggle of small children who had gathered in the village square where they had alighted.

Their faces were curious, their expressions innocent. Far too innocent to hear the curse word he had been about to utter into the bright spring morning.

"Ah," Henry said. "Yes. Good morning."

The children scattered. Evidently strangers were unusual in Pathstow.

"It'll come right off, Your Grace, I am sure," said Jenks briskly, glancing at the muck streaked up his master's boot.

Henry sighed and tried to find a patch of grass on the village green to wipe his boot. Stamping away from his servant gave him a moment to collect his thoughts. Something he had not done much of in the last four and twenty hours...perhaps to his peril.

The dark sky was streaked with gold as mist steamed off the fields around the small village. A rooster crowed somewhere in the pokey gardens of the houses smaller than his entrance hallway at Dulverton Manor. There was the overwhelming sense that a person, once born in Pathstow, likely never left.

Henry scraped his boot mercilessly against the grass and was gratified to see the muck removed.

Well, at least that was one thing that had gone his way today...

His dark eyes scanned the square where his driver had stopped. Dear God, to think this place was a hundred miles from his home. From all the comforts a duke could expect. From the respect, nay, almost worship his tenants gave him.

The suspicious look a farmer gave him as he rode past on a carthorse was nothing like the bowing and scraping Henry was accustomed to receiving.

Yet he could not help but be curious. Pathstow was unlike any place he had ever been. More like a dream of the English countryside than what he had expected in reality.

I've spent more time in London in the last year than out of it, Henry thought ruefully.

That was where he would rather be. In the Dulverton townhouse in Knightsbridge, or at the Dulverton Club—named after a distant ancestor, it now offered life membership to anyone in the family.

Lord, even simpering at Almack's would be better than this.

Henry sighed as he looked once more at his boot. It would never be the same again.

But there was nothing for it. After putting up with the damned scandal for weeks, he would abide it no longer. If he could not find—

"I really will be able to treat the stain, Your Grace," said Jenks reproachfully from the carriage. "You do not have to concern yourself with such things."

Henry strode back to the carriage. "I suppose you are offended by my meager attempts, Jenks?"

"Not offended, Your Grace, merely conscious of their inadequacy," said his manservant blithely.

Henry snorted. Well, he had always striven for honesty with his servants, but perhaps honesty could go too far. "Thank you, Jenks."

"My pleasure, Your Grace."

"Well, what do you think?"

The manservant tilted his head. "I am not sure my employment requires me to be given to much thinking, Your Grace."

Henry sighed heavily and spread his arms wide. "Pathstow. Your thoughts?"

It had been remarkably difficult to discover the location in the first place, Henry thought darkly, *and we could still be wrong.*

After all, the headlines printed in that damned newspaper, *The Courier*, hardly proclaimed where they were getting their information. It would hardly be good for business.

But day after day, week after week, the pages declared the most outrageous slander about his sister, and he had had enough.

Lady Margaret Everleigh shocks ton by meeting secretly with lover

Lady Margaret Everleigh suspected to be with child

Hushed up Dulverton scandal rocks Society…

Henry's jaw tightened at the very remembrance of the outrageous things he had been forced to read in that damned rag. It was outrageous! It was criminal!

With every passing day, he had demanded to see the editor. Each time, the scrawny little man had laughed and pointed out there was little the duke could do.

"My sources are protected, Your Grace, and there is nothing you can do to procure them," he had said with barely hidden glee. "What I decide to print is my business."

3

"And my sister is mine to protect," Henry had snarled, barely able to keep his fists to himself, the provocation was so absolute. "And I will not permit you to—"

"Permit me?" The editor had snickered. "You seem to be under the mistaken illusion that you and your kind run the world, Your Grace. You may be rich, have a duchy, stride up and down Rotten Row as though you are the king of the world, but this is a new century, may I remind you. The people have a little more power now."

Henry snorted, his breath billowing in the crisp morning air of Pathstow. *The cheek of the man!*

"Tell me again, Your Grace," said Jenks delicately.

The question made little sense. "Tell you what?"

Henry had attempted not to snap, but he was sore pushed. Upon discovering their destination, there had been little time for preparations. He had merely bundled a few things that might be useful into a carriage, including Jenks, and rushed off into the night.

Perhaps I would be in a better temper if I had slept...

"Tell me what we are doing here," his manservant said delicately.

Henry glared for a moment, but seeing no insolence in his servant's air, spoke heavily. "Well, you know the awful things being printed about Lady Margaret."

Jenks's eyebrow raised. "Once I saw the first headline, Your Grace, I can assure you we burnt the thing in the kitchen and have not read the newspaper since."

And that, Henry thought, his head lifting higher, *was the value of a good servant.*

"I assume, however, that my distaste for the lies did not prevent additional printing?"

Henry's temple pulsed painfully. "No, I am afraid it did not. Worse, the newspaper started to print further lies about other ladies of Society—ladies of good name and repute. All false, naturally."

"Naturally."

He glared once more at his manservant, attempting to find any hint of sarcasm, but there was none. Jenks's face was calm yet slightly fierce, as though an offense against Lady Margaret—Peg, to her brother—was an offense against them all.

Which in a way, Henry supposed, *it was.*

"The damned editor wouldn't give me a single iota of information about their source," said Henry darkly, watching curtains being drawn in the houses around the village square. "But a little gold carefully spent about the place threw up two vital pieces of information."

"One of them, presumably, this village."

Henry nodded. By God, he should be in London right now. His friend Penshaw had been gone for a good while, and he had promised the man that when he was gone—to the Continent, Henry assumed— he would look in on Penshaw's sister.

Which was partly why he was here. It was bad enough his own sister was victim to these outrageous slanders, but he was around to protect her, protect her reputation.

But what about Penshaw's sister? *How many sisters had to be slandered before the damned thing stopped?*

"And the second?"

Henry breathed in heavily. There was a new scent upon the morning air. Wood burning, yes, but also something else. Something sharp. Something that reminded him of the stables, when…

Ah, yes.

"The gossip is being spread from a household here," Henry said darkly. "Part of a network, apparently. We're only fifteen miles from London, a fast horse could make that distance in a day. This is where it's coming from."

Jenks did not look so convinced. He glanced around, his lip curling at the genteel poverty that surrounded them. "Here?"

Henry nodded.

He had hardly believed it himself when the first report had been brought to him. But after the fifth, he had no choice but to believe it.

Mr. Banfield. That was the man they were here to find. It was he who spread the rumors—no, it was worse than that. He who was fabricating lies, desecrating the reputation of eligible young ladies.

He would call the blaggard out, meet him tomorrow at dawn with pistols, shoot the man, and that would be an end to it.

A smile curled Henry's lip. Why, he may even be able to return to London that day. He could be back in the comfort his title demanded within six and thirty hours.

"And you are going to—"

"Take care of it," Henry snarled.

The bitterness coursing through his veins made any other tone impossible. Well, how dare the wretch Banfield do such a thing? How much money had the fool been paid? Did he have any idea what a risk he was taking, playing with the innocence of the *ton's* finest flowers?

"Ah," said Jenks helplessly. "Take care of it."

Henry nodded. The day was warming swiftly. There would not be much time to carry out his...well, one could not precisely call it a plan. Not if it took less than a heartbeat to create.

"And you intend to do this by...?"

"I am absolutely certain the gossip—the lies about my sister originate from this village," said Henry darkly, running a hand through his hair. *God, he would have to sleep soon.* "From one place in particular."

His manservant's gaze was drawn to the manor just to their left, outside the village. It sat atop a hill, leaning over Pathstow.

Manor. Henry almost laughed aloud. It was nothing to Dulverton Manor, but these parochial places never were. Some baronet whose great-great-grandfather was in the right place at the right time for a monarch a century ago, and who now spent their time crowing over their neighbors, no doubt.

"You would think so, wouldn't you?" Henry said quietly, as a few women passed, heavy burdens of laundry baskets resting against their hips. "But no, it is not the local gentry who has started to put these nasty rumors about."

Jenks's eyes widened. "No?"

Henry shook his head. "No. Believe it or not, the miscreant who I will be dealing with is…the blacksmith."

He almost laughed at the surprise in his servant's face. It was a rather wild suggestion. If he had not received the same news time and time again from multiple sources from London's streets, he would not have credited it himself.

"Yes, this Banfield has messages coming and going, all very secret," Henry said quietly, his heart thundering at the injustice. "That's where I'm going."

"Going?"

It was perhaps a foolish idea, even Henry had to admit. Why, he was a duke, though no one in this small village knew that. There would be no magistrate here, probably. No justice who could stand his ground alongside him.

No one to protect him if things got ugly.

Henry drew himself up. But he would not need anyone to stand beside him and protect him. An Everleigh, needing protection?

Not a chance.

"You are sure about this?" For some reason, Jenks's face looked worried. "I mean to say, Your Grace, these allegations are most serious, and unsubstantiated—I do not mean you are acting in bad faith," he added hurriedly.

He had evidently seen Henry's glower. "Are you suggesting I am incorrect, Jenks?"

"I would never say such a thing to you, Your Grace."

"That's right—" Henry paused as his mind caught up.

Jenks radiated an expression of pure innocence, which was impressive for a man nearing forty with a reputation ten years ago, Henry had been informed, of a few seductions in the nearby town to Dulverton Manor.

"Yes. Well. Precisely. But tell me this, Jenks. What would you do if

I could present you with the man who had attempted to sully Lady Margaret's reputation?"

The jovial and innocent expression disappeared immediately from the servant's face. "Am I permitted a weapon, Your Grace, or will I need to use my bare hands?"

Henry grinned. "Precisely. Here, give me a hand with this."

He moved so swiftly around the carriage, the manservant was on the backfoot. Henry had already thrown open the door and pulled from beneath the seat the trunk he had placed there when they had left Dulverton Manor.

It was not large. It did not need to be.

"Quickly man, before the rest of Pathstow wakes up," he hissed under his breath, excitement rushing through his veins.

He shouldn't be enjoying this. He wasn't, really. He was only here to avenge his sister's honor and make completely sure no such nonsense would appear in the newspapers.

The very idea of those stories being true! It was incomprehensible!

Which was why it was wild that his heart beat excitedly.

It was not as though much excitement happened in his life, Henry tried to tell himself as his fingers fumbled with the trunk's clasp. The war in France was almost over, that's what they kept saying, and much of his life was taken up with reviewing rental surveys and mediating arguments between servants.

Dull dinners, boring balls, and catatonic card parties were all London could offer.

No, this was an adventure, Henry thought as he started to pull the clothes from the trunk. Two days in Pathstow, a little light revenge, and he could return to the Dulverton Club with a hilarious story that would impress.

"B-But Your Grace!"

The outraged horror in Jenks's voice made Henry smile. Really, he could not have hoped for a better reception to the jacket he was holding.

"Help me off with mine, Jenks," he said to his manservant, trying to shrug off the heavy elegant woolen creation of the finest tailor in York as he clambered into the carriage. It was not the perfect dressing room, but it would do. "Come on!"

"But, but," stammered Jenks as he rushed to help his master out of coat, waistcoat, shirt, and breeches. "I don't understand!"

"Good," Henry said cheerfully as he pulled on the stained, slightly torn, and much mended clothes he had pulled from the trunk. "If you would not expect a duke to be so dressed, then we shall have to hope old Banfield won't either."

"But Your Grace, where on earth did you find such offensive garments?"

It was difficult not to laugh. Henry had never heard such disdain drip from his manservant's voice. True, the clothes were rather careworn, but that was the whole point, wasn't it?

A duke was in danger unless he was in disguise...

"One of the undergardeners was getting married, and I promised him an entire new set of clothes if he gave me his," explained Henry, as though this was perfectly natural behavior of a duke. "He can't complain, I'll treat him to a full suit from George Stulz from Savile Row."

"Your Grace!"

"Oh, Jenks, don't give me that," Henry said, stepping out of the carriage and breathing in the air of Pathstow as though he were a new man.

The manservant staggered from the carriage, legs barely able to hold him as he stared in horror at his master. "Your Grace!"

"That's Everleigh to you," Henry corrected.

Well, it was rather a clever idea. Of course the blacksmith would never admit to his perfidy if he just strode in there wearing the trappings of wealth and privilege.

No, he had to go in there and wheedle the truth out of him. And wouldn't it be easier for the man to admit his guilt if he believed he was doing so to another man of his own class? Another blacksmith, say?

"B-But Your Grace!" Jenks was still spluttering as Henry started walking toward the scent of wood and iron on the air. "Where will you stay? What will you do for—"

"I've got a few guineas, I'll take a room in one of the pubs." Henry had been pleased with his foresight until he saw his manservant's face.

"One of the pubs?" Jenks said, bewildered. "Your Grace, there is but one!"

Nothing the man said could dissuade Henry from his purpose. He had to save Peg's reputation, didn't he? Not to mention the other reputations easily ruined by such malevolent lies. That meant accosting Banfield.

He had thought of everything.

"Oh, don't worry so much, Jenks," said Henry with a grin. "Take the carriage back to London and await me there. Don't tell anyone, and I'll be back in a few days. How hard can it be?"

Ignoring his manservant's continued splutters, Henry strode forward with purpose. The day was warming with every passing minute, and it was not hard to follow the sound of hammering that now accosted his ears.

The smithy. A crucial part of any village, he knew. The hammering was steady, continuous, evidently delivered by a well-practiced hand.

Henry stretched his shoulders as he walked, just in case the man lashed out as soon as he asked about the gossip. The smithy was right before him, door open and heat pouring out.

For just a moment, Henry paused and reminded himself why he was here. Peg had to be protected, and he was the only one who knew the scandals were coming from here.

Banfield may wish to fight, but that was fine by Henry. His fingers itched to mete out vengeance. He stretched his hands, curling them into fists as he strode into the smithy. One could never tell. One had to be prepared for—

"What do *you* want?"

Henry's jaw fell open, and he came to an ungainly halt.

The smithy was large, far larger than he had initially supposed. There were racks of instruments, a bench covered in what must be the smithy's day's work. A huge furnace on one side of the room was pumping out so much heat, his brow immediately began to swelter.

But that was not what had disquieted him. Standing by the forge and over the anvil was a woman.

Not just a woman. A *woman*. Henry had never seen the like, and he'd been met a fair few of the ladies of the *ton*.

She was…beautiful, was the only way to describe her. Dark hair, almost raven black, swept up in a messy knot that certainly wouldn't have passed muster at Almack's. Her hips and breasts swelled under a leather apron tied behind her back, and the warmth of the room made her skin glow.

There was also a glare in her eyes.

"Well?" she snapped, pushing back her hair. "I said, what do you want?"

Henry closed his mouth hastily. This was foolishness. He had not come here to be dazzled by the wife of Banfield, he was here to accost Banfield himself.

The last thing he needed to be doing was gawping at the man's wife, trying not to look too carefully at the glistening skin, the curve of her—

"Sir?"

"Y-Yes," Henry said hurriedly, forcing the distraction away. "Yes, I…I wish to see Banfield."

The woman raised an imperious eyebrow. "Well?"

EMILY E K MURDOCH

He swallowed. *Of course, he should have been specific.* "Mr. Banfield. The blacksmith, the owner of this place."

Why was his heart thundering so powerfully? Why was his concentration—

The woman smiled, such a mischievous expression that Henry's stomach dropped painfully to his feet.

"The blacksmith?" she said archly. "You've found her."

CHAPTER TWO

MINNY BANFIELD CAREFULLY laid down the scalding hot chisel as a tall, broad figure stumbled into the forge.

Well, this was a strange to-do. A stranger. Not someone from the village. She had lived here all her life and knew every family, every face.

"What do *you* want?" she asked briskly, looking carefully at him.

The man's jaw fell open in a surprisingly slipshod manner.

A small smile crept across Minny's face. It happened fairly regularly. The road to London had been improved awhile back. Every now and again, you'd find a soul wander in after having a few drinks at the King's Head.

Just looking, they would say, curiosity gleaming in their eyes. Townies, never seen a smithy before in their lives.

And then there were ones like these. Fools, the lot of them, come to gawp at her. Likely as not he'd heard tell of her in the pub, Minny thought darkly, her smile disappearing as the idiot just kept staring.

"Well?" she snapped, pushing back her hair. "I said, what do you want?"

The least he could do was ask her a question—*or give her a commission, all the better*, Minny thought wearily. Trade hadn't been what it was. The world preferred to buy new now, rather than mend the tools which had served them for so long.

Minny pushed back her hair again and wished she had not been working so carefully on a delicate piece of work, still lying on the anvil. It would be cooling now, and it had taken her almost twenty minutes to get the thing to the right temperature.

Worse, the man's gaze was starting to play merry havoc with her heart.

He was handsome. Oh, she tried not to notice, but even poor clothes could not hide the strength beneath that coat or the handsome cut of his jaw.

Minny ignored it as best she could, the sticky glistening of her skin, skin that had worked hard all morning—far earlier than this man had been up, she'd be bound—and wondered whether he was just planning to stand there forever.

She waited another minute, then glanced at the belt buckle on the anvil. She'd need to start again. *Oh, this was ridiculous!*

"Sir?" she said testily.

"Y-Yes?" The man blinked a few times, as though he had never seen a woman before in his life. Then he seemed to pull himself together. "Yes, I...I wish to see Banfield."

Ah, one who hadn't heard then. Minny was going to enjoy this. There was a dark pleasure in proving to the world at large and to a man in particular that she was the one who worked the bellows here.

Doing her best to ape the imperious tone of a lady she had once seen, Minny said, "Well?"

The man swallowed. Minny watched his Adam's apple bob, drawing her attention back to his taut jawline and the mere hint of stubble that had grown overnight.

"Mr. Banfield. The blacksmith, the owner of this place."

Minny grinned. *Oh, this was perfect. One day,* she thought, *a man would not say such things, expect such things, presume to know what belonged to a woman.*

He hadn't learned so far, but she would teach him.

"The blacksmith?" she said archly. "You've found her."

It was unfortunate that the man looked so utterly flabbergasted.

Was it not obvious, Minny thought irritably as she turned to pump up the bellows, not wishing to lose any of the blaze's heat, *that she was the owner?*

Who else would be here, standing over the anvil?

But she did not have time to worry about handsome—*about tiresome men,* Minny corrected in the privacy of her mind. She had work to do, precious work she had almost begged for at the neighboring farms and the big house.

If she wanted to keep her reputation, keep the forge blazing, then she did not wish to deliver her work late.

"Now, if you'll excuse—"

"No, I meant the owner of the forge," said the man slowly, as though she was hard of thinking as well as hard of hearing. "The blacksmith."

Minny permitted herself a tight grin. "Yes, I understood you perfectly."

"Then where is he?" The man looked around, eyes curious.

It took all her self-control merely to take in a slow, deep breath, and fix her smile even though she wished to scowl.

Being interrupted was one thing. Being interrupted by handsome men, well, that was another. But to be interrupted by a damned fool who would not listen to a word she said?

Oh, that would not be born.

"I meant," Minny said as calmly as she could manage, "that I am the owner. Is that so difficult to understand?"

Of course it was. She was being ridiculous, she knew, but that knowledge did little to quiet the bitter rage rushing through her.

It was so unfair. The world expected a man in such a field. *The world expected a man in every field,* Minny thought darkly. The idea of a woman doing a man's job...well, it was unthinkable.

One only had to look at the incredulity on the man's face before her to see that.

It was a shame, too. Minny was not usually one to have her head turned by a handsome face—though that could be because she knew all the handsome faces in Pathstow, and they were all either spoken for or terrible womanizers.

Not something she was interested in.

The spectacle of a handsome man she did not know was rather a surprise. It altered the monotony of heat, hard work, and exhaustion.

Though if he did not swiftly reassess his statements, he was going to find himself out on his ear...

The expression of astonishment had not disappeared from the man's face. "My name is Henry Everleigh, and I demand to see the blacksmith."

Minny sighed and turned her back on the man to work up the bellows again. *A hopeless case, then. One of these days,* she told herself, *she would discover a man willing to suspend his disbelief for more than five minutes. Then they would see just what she could do.*

Until then, she would simply have to put up with these nincom-poops.

"If you don't mind, I am incredibly busy," she said sharply, turning back to the anvil and picking up a hammer.

Bending over the solid iron, Minny narrowed her eyes at the part of the broken buckle. You saw it all the time with this weak London work, you needed something far more hardwearing if you wished to hand it down to your daughter.

True, she would admit that the lattice work was rather fine. Nothing to what she could create of course, but that would make it all the easier to mend.

Was the furnace hot enough yet?

"But—but you cannot possibly be the owner!"

Minny sighed and glanced at the man who was showing no sign of leaving or learning. "And why is that?"

Mr. Everleigh opened his mouth, closed it again, then spluttered, "B-But you can't be?"

"Why?" Minny asked as sweetly as she could manage.

Her attention returned to the belt buckle as she rammed the hammer into the furnace to heat up. No, it wouldn't take long to mend this, perhaps another hour? Then she could move onto the three sickles old Mr.—

"You just can't," said Mr. Everleigh helplessly, despite all evidence to the contrary.

Minny sighed as she pulled the hammer from the fire and leaned over the belt buckle. "Are women forbidden to own property?"

It appeared the handsome—*no, the irritating,* she corrected herself—man had not expected that.

"Well of course they can—"

"And women can work," Minny interrupted, carefully beating out the breakage in the belt as she allowed the metal to soften. Delicate work at the best of times, and she did not need a blundering idiot—

"Yes, I suppose so—"

"And I am the one working, right now, in the forge, at the anvil, in the smithy," Minny said as calmly as she could manage. "Like a blacksmith."

Irritation was blossoming through her body, growing hotter with each passing moment. The forge was always boiling, always unbearably hot, especially in the summer. Which was why it did not help that when she grew irritated—when that Banfield temper threatened to rear its head—she grew even hotter. Every moment that passed, she could feel her temper starting to loosen its chains.

She needed to concentrate. Minny dropped her gaze to her work. That was what she should be thinking of.

That was the trouble with smithing; when one had intricate work, one's own breath could warm or cool the metal to an intolerable temperature. Concentration was absolutely—

"It does not follow, my good woman, that you are the—"

"I am not," Minny snapped, pushed beyond all endurance, "your good woman!"

She straightened, fiercely glaring at the man who had stepped forward, seemingly unconsciously, to see what she was working on.

She had also pointed at Mr. Everleigh in her anger. This would have been quite acceptable in most circles—well, if not acceptable, at least expected.

He was abominably rude, after all.

The trouble was, this was not most circles. This was a smithy. And she was holding—

"Good God, woman!"

"Sorry," Minny said hastily, placing the white hot hammer back on the anvil. "I did not mean—"

"You could have had my eye out with that!"

"Only," said Minny with a dark grin, "with very great care."

For a moment, silence hung in the air.

Well. Other than the thundering of her own pulse in her ears, the roaring of the furnace, and the quiet crackle of the metal on the anvil cooling.

Mr. Everleigh was staring. Minny could feel his gaze burning into her just as fiercely as if she had dropped the hammer on her skin.

No man had ever looked at her like that, as though he was prodding through her mind in an attempt to eke out a secret.

As though attempting to make a decision.

Minny sighed. Well, she was not about to permit a potential customer to walk through that door thinking she had intended to hurt him, no matter how it had looked.

"I am sorry," she said stiffly. "I...forgot I was holding the hammer."

Mr. Everleigh frowned. "I thought you said you were a blacksmith?"

Minny's hands trembled by her sides, but she did not permit herself to sink into the temper she had languished in when a child.

Fighting in scraps was all very well for a chit of eight years old, but a woman of more than twenty should know better.

Probably.

"That's as may be," she said stiffly. She needed to cool down…easier said than done in a forge. "Still, I am sorry for it. Good morning, sir."

Picking up the hammer, Minny examined it for a moment, then immediately thrust it back into the forge. Another reheating. If her father could see her now—

"You *are* the blacksmith, aren't you?" came the curious voice behind her.

Minny rolled her eyes. *Men. And they thought they had the superior intelligence!*

"However did you work that out?" she asked sweetly as she turned back to the anvil and the waiting belt buckle.

"Ah," said Mr. Everleigh helplessly. "In that case, it is my turn to apologize."

"Yes, I rather think that it is," Minny said. "But as I have much work to do and only one pair of hands, I will save you the trouble of shaking mine and merely recommend the door right behind you."

She dropped her gaze to the belt buckle and tried not to permit disappointment to seep into her heart.

She was being foolish. No man who looked like that would fail to find female admirers. He was here because he was nosey, passing through no doubt, and would soon be gone.

And the village of Pathstow, Minny thought with a wry grin, *would be better off without him.* Less pleasing to look at, but—

"You're still here," Minny could not help but say as she gently teased the glowing metal into a more pleasing shape.

"You are an intelligent woman."

It was a great effort to prevent herself from rolling her eyes again. *Well, really.* Any man thought a little gentle flattery would get them everywhere. Perhaps it would have done, if he had not been so irritating when he had first come in.

Minny did not look up. "Doesn't take a genius to notice no steps were taken. You can go, you know."

"I don't want to go. I came here to find the blacksmith."

Why was there such a curious tone in his voice? Oh, Minny knew many people were curious about her taking over the smithy. Outsiders, that was. Villagers knew her, knew her father, knew the name. It was unusual, yes, but it was Minny.

But this man, this Mr. Everleigh's voice was more than curious. It suggested he had many questions and would refuse to take no for an answer.

A strange sort of curiosity curled around her own heart. What was a man like him doing here? Why could he possibly have come to find the owner of this forge? There was no bundle on him, nothing that could require mending.

Perhaps he had a commission for her.

Minny tried to force the excitement from her chest. That would be too much to hope for. Commissions were where the money was, and she had never received one. Seen her father accept them, of course, but never been offered one.

Perhaps he wanted a silversmith, a recommendation. Perhaps he was lost. No, that didn't make sense; he could have asked anyone directions.

"What do you want?" she said finally, frowning as she concentrated on the last little hit of her hammer that would finish the belt off.

"I want to learn smithing."

It was fortunate indeed that Minny had lifted her hand at that moment, rather than tried to finish off the complex work. She would have ruined the belt, such was the jolting surprise that rushed through her arm and shoulder at his words.

"I want to learn smithing."

Minny straightened and looked straight into Mr. Everleigh's eyes.

And gasped. It was swiftly stifled, and thankfully her cheeks were already red thanks to the glowing forge.

There was nothing but blazing honesty in that man's eyes.

He truly wished to learn. He wanted to be here, at the very least. Minny had never seen such an expression of determination in anyone—save perhaps, herself. She had a looking glass, a small one, inherited from her mother. She had seen in Mr. Everleigh's eyes the same look she'd had when she had taken over the forge.

Absolute determination. The expectation of getting her own way. A complete denial of all other opinions.

It was like seeing someone across a crowded room and suddenly knowing, knowing that person was important.

She could not explain it. Minny was not even sure she had the vocabulary for it.

But it was impossible. Reason rushed back into her mind as she blinked, staring at the handsome Mr. Everleigh. No, given her...other activities, there was no possibility of risking having a stranger about the place.

Besides, she needed to concentrate on her own smithing. She needed to build up the business, create the best work possible. How was she supposed to do that while teaching?

Teaching, Minny could not help but think, *a handsome man who had already proved to be far too much of a distraction...*

"No," she said firmly.

"I am afraid I do not usually take no for an answer," said Mr. Everleigh lightly.

A smile quirked Minny's lips. "Well, then, I am glad to give you a change of pace."

He laughed, but the laughter faded as he saw her resolute expression. "You are in earnest."

"Never more so," said Minny.

The belt was finished. She could move it in a moment and polish it later. Then start with the sickles next, though there was a set of horseshoes already paid for that—

"I am sorry, Miss Banfield, but I must insist," said Mr. Everleigh slowly, stepping forward.

He could come no further, there was an anvil between them, and Minny found herself rather glad of that fact.

He was a strong man, this Mr. Everleigh, not only in body but in mind. If he placed those firm fingers on her arms in an attempt to persuade her, she was not sure what she would do…

Scandalous thoughts cascaded through her mind.

Minny pushed them away, cheeks surely flushing with embarrassment. *The very idea of her letting him touch her!*

"I want to learn smithing," Mr. Everleigh insisted.

"Go into any forge in the country," Minny said, her mouth dry. "They'll teach you."

"It has to be you."

He was mad! Why on earth did he want her?

Not want her, Minny thought swiftly. *Not want her, precisely.*

"I have been told Banfield is the best blacksmith outside London," Mr. Everleigh was saying. "And I wish to learn from the best."

A prickle of irritation made Minny say, "Best in London, too, I'll be bound."

"Well, there you are then," said Mr. Everleigh triumphantly. "I will simply have to learn from you."

Minny cursed herself for falling so swiftly into his trap. Perhaps he wasn't a complete dolt after all—but that did not mean that she would risk her secret being exposed by having a man about the place!

"I can pay you."

She swallowed and glanced into the knowing eyes of the man before her. Money would certainly be useful, lessen the pressure, as it were.

But she could not take such a risk. No. Tempting as this man and his offer were, she simply would not jeopardize it.

"I am sorry, Mr. Everleigh, but there is no apprentice position available at my forge," Minny said sweetly. "Goodbye."

"But—"

"I said," Minny repeated, picking up her hammer, coming around the anvil, and pushing the man toward the door. "Goodbye."

With a great shove Mr. Everleigh had evidently not been expecting, Minny pushed him onto the pavement and slammed the door behind her.

Then she leaned against the door and tried to catch her breath. *Well! Had any woman ever been so tempted?*

CHAPTER THREE

April 1, 1810

"AND YOU SAY she truly is the blacksmith?" Henry could not help but say.

It was all he could do to keep the incredulity from his voice as he paid for his breakfast—a bowl of porridge that looked as though it had already passed through a dog.

"Oh yes, Minny's been our blacksmith for a year or more, ain't she, Ted?" nodded the wife of the owner of the King's Head.

Henry had managed to find a room there yesterday afternoon after meandering around Pathstow in a state of absolute confusion.

"Find a room." He had been forced to haggle with Ted, the only name the owner went by, for near on ten minutes before agreeing on a price. Only then did the man admit, gleefully, that the place was empty.

"But a woman!" Henry said in astonishment. "A woman black-smith!"

Ted raised a grizzled eyebrow. "You don't have women with brains back in London?"

Henry flushed. It was bad enough to find himself on the back foot in Pathstow, particularly when he wished to impress Banfield, then call him out for his outrageous behavior. It had been awkward having that blasted conversation with Minny—with Miss Banfield yesterday.

She could have knocked him down with a feather when she had revealed she was the owner of that forge...

But the last thing he needed was some country bumpkin acting as though Pathstow was the peak of tolerance!

"I am well aware that women have brains, thank you, *Mr. Ted*," Henry said coldly.

He saw the surprise on the older man's face for just a few moments before realizing he was not, at the King's Head, the Duke of Dulverton.

No, he was plain old Mr. Henry Everleigh. That meant he could not go around chastising people for their opinions, even if they were ridiculous.

Henry swallowed. It was going to take a great deal of getting used to.

"I just meant," he said, leaning against the bar in the empty pub, "I did not expect a woman to be doing such a...well. A man's job."

Ted's raised grizzled eyebrow was joined by its partner. "You think a woman isn't strong enough, then?"

Henry winced at the memory of Minny—of Miss Banfield's thrusting hand that had shoved him out of the forge. He would have that bruise for a month.

"No," he conceded.

It was very strange. Precisely why he had been so shocked was obvious; women did not run forges. Women were not blacksmiths. It was just one of those things everyone knew.

The trouble was, now he was sitting and thinking about it, Henry could not exactly explain why. "It had always been that way" did not appear to be a sufficient response, even in the privacy of his own mind.

His jaw tightened.

"I have been told Banfield is the best blacksmith outside London. And I wish to learn from the best."

She had sounded certain when she had refused him, but he could not just abandon his plan. Coming all the way to Pathstow wasn't something a gentleman did lightly, and he had his sister to think of. Peg would find her reputations ruined if scandalous lies were once again printed in that rag.

He had to go back to the forge, Henry realized with a sinking heart. *He would have to talk to Miss Banfield again and convince her, that was all.*

"You're going back there, aren't you?"

Henry saw the knowing grin of the pub landlord. "What of it?"

Ted nodded sagely. "A few young men have gone to that forge over the year. Plenty of young men, now I come to think about it."

A slither of rage, of jealous madness entered Henry's heart, but he pushed it out as swiftly as it had come.

What was he thinking! He was no father nor brother to defend Miss Banfield's honor.

No, Henry thought darkly. *The feelings he had for Minny were absolutely nothing like those of a brother…*

"Yes," he said aloud. "I am sure there are plenty of men that visit Miss Banfield."

Was this not the evidence he needed? Why else would men be going to the Pathstow forge all the time, if not to pass messages between her and the newspaper in London?

How Miss Banfield had managed to get herself entangled in such nonsense, Henry could not say. But that was not his concern. His concern was Peggy, his sister, and all the potential suitors she would lose if this nonsense continued much longer.

No, he would have to harden his heart to Minny—*damn, Miss Banfield*—and convince her, somehow, to teach him. The closer he was to the forge, the easier it would be to discover evidence of her dealings with this network. He already had an idea that would change her mind.

"You say hullo to that girl," said Ted quietly, leaving the bar and walking to a door to the kitchens. "She's a good girl. Like her father."

Henry nodded. Perhaps she was, but that had not prevented her from getting enmeshed in a scandal that would break once he had the evidence, by God.

The forge was already alight, though the hour was early. Henry supposed that here, as for the servants at Dulverton Manor, work began when the sun came up. It was nearing summer with every passing day.

He breathed in deeply as he stopped just outside the blacksmith's. There was something darkly intoxicating about the smoke that billowed from the chimney. Perhaps he was imagining it, but there seemed to be another scent there, mingled with the wood and iron.

Something that made him think of a woman's glistening skin, the way her chest heaved as her frustration grew…

Henry swallowed. If he was going to make this work, he would have to get a grip on himself. No admiring the woman who was destroying his sister's reputation. No daydreaming about what it would be like to pull the irritating woman into his arms and stop her protests with a heady kiss.

No. All he had to do was convince a woman, who evidently had no desire to ever set eyes on him again, to take him into her confidence.

As simple as that.

Henry took a deep breath and stepped once more into the forge.

It was stifling hot, much as it had been yesterday—and just like yesterday, his attention was almost immediately taken by the woman standing by the anvil.

Well, standing. Staggering was perhaps a more accurate description.

Without hesitation, without even thinking about whether Minny Banfield would welcome such assistance, Henry lunged forward.

The heavy plough in her hands was slipping, her fingers curling around the edge insufficient to hold it in place, but the moment Henry took the other side, it steadied.

He heard, rather than saw, the heavy sigh.

"Thank God," came Minny's voice. "I had thought myself quite up to the task, but I believe I had underestimated its full weight—over here, on the bench, if you do not mind."

It was remarkably heavy. Henry marveled, back straining and shoulders crying out, at how she had managed to pick the thing up in the first place. It took all his strength to carry it with her over to the bench.

With a groan, Henry placed the plough carefully onto the bench. It was a relief to let go, his fingers aching immediately from the heavy load.

"There," came Minny's grateful voice. "Thank you, Mr....oh. It's you."

Henry's heart sank. Just for a moment, the two of them had been united. Struggling toward the same goal.

But she was not the only one disappointed. His foolish heart had already begun imagining something ridiculous…

Which was impossible. Was he not here because Miss Banfield, who looked all innocent and beautiful and—*innocent*, Henry caught himself just in time. But who was not innocent in the slightest.

Lady Margaret Everleigh shocks ton by meeting secretly with lover…

Lady Margaret Everleigh suspected to be with child…

Hushed up Dulverton scandal rocks Society…

Henry swallowed the bitter ire that rose as he remembered the headlines which had attempted to slander his sister.

Anyone who could help concoct such fanciful, ruinous stories was not innocent and was certainly not someone he could work with.

Against, yes. But not as partners.

"I told you yesterday, I have no time for an apprentice," scowled Minny, her words meaningless as Henry tried not to look at her flushed cheeks and parted lips.

Damnit.

"I have no wish to be indentured as an apprentice, so that is all to the good," said Henry to Minny's back as she returned to the anvil. "I merely wish to—"

"I said no. Doesn't a man like you understand a woman when she says no?"

She could not have injured him any more greatly if she had stuck that sickle hanging on the wall right through his chest.

Henry staggered back. To suggest to a gentleman, to a duke no less, that he would be so dishonorable as to ignore a woman's wishes!

He hesitated, mind rushing to catch up with his disgruntled sense of decency.

Ah. Except, he thought wildly as Minny pumped the bellows, causing a roar of flame to echo around the forge, *he was ignoring her wishes.* And he was a gentleman, a duke, a member of Society...but she did not know that.

It had been a mistake, really, to tell her his real name. But then, how many people outside of London knew the Duke of Dulverton's surname was not Dulverton, but Everleigh?

"I know it is April Fool's Day," said Minny with a laugh, "but I thought you the fool yesterday. Are you just a permanent fool?"

"That I am not," Henry said, jaw tightening.

Time to take back control of this situation—as much as he could. Perhaps he would be far better off returning to London and sending an agent in his stead. Someone who knew the first thing about black-smithing, for example. Or not being a duke.

But he couldn't leave now. Something he could not explain drew him toward Minny Banfield—*what sort of a name was Minny, anyway?*—and he could not leave her.

Could not leave the forge, Henry hastily corrected himself. Could not leave the possibility of uncovering the truth of these lies. Could not return to London, tail between his legs, to admit he had been unable to decipher the source of such mischief.

Henry drew himself up. No, if he was going to challenge Minny

Banfield on her outrageous behavior, then he had to do something he did rarely, and loathed when the time came to do it.

"I must apologize," he said stiffly.

Minny gave him not a single glance. "Yes, I suppose you must."

That was not the response he had been expecting.

A muscle twitched in Henry's jaw. "I must?"

"You were the one who said that," she pointed out, taking a sickle from the wall and examining it. "Not I."

Was it the smithy or the blacksmith's presence tying his tongue in knots, making every thought dart in random directions?

"I should not have been so presumptuous," Henry began again.

At the word "presumptuous," Minny looked up in surprise.

Ah. Right. He was supposed to be a relatively unlettered, uncouth sort of chap, with no idea what manners were, let alone how to address an earl, a viscount, and a major around a table of whist.

He tried again. "I should not have been a complete ass."

Minny stifled a laugh. The sight of her grinning made Henry's stomach twist in a far too delicious way.

Do not get distracted, man.

"I should have seen the talent with which you operate—you hit things," Henry adjusted once again. "Besides, I have asked about the village, and you are held in very high repute. For a woman."

There was another stifled laugh. "I am delighted to find you have discovered I am acceptable. For a woman."

Henry silently cursed his foolish tongue. "You know what I mean."

"I suppose I do," said Minny, laying the sickle on the anvil before placing her hands on her hips and examining him. "You're saying you were an ass, an idiot, a fool of the greatest degree, a moron who refused to listen to what a woman told him, then refused to believe the truth his own eyes showed him. Is that it?"

Henry swallowed a significant amount of pride. "Yes."

Minny's hair shone in the firelight sparking from the furnace, and it was that which drew his attention as he waited in silence.

That, and the way her hands softly sank into the curves of her hips. *Damnit man, you ought to be concentrating!*

"Well," she said softly, evidently mollified. "That's better. I am glad to see some sense can be forced into that brain of yours."

Henry tried not to think how swiftly his Cambridge dons would have agreed with her, and pushed forward with his advantage. "Wonderful. Now you can—"

"I am not teaching you the ways of the forge," said Minny with a heavy sense of finality. "Good day, sir."

Her attention slipped once more from him to the sickle. It was ridiculous really, he thought wretchedly. Envious of a lump of metal.

But he could not help it. He wanted to be examined by Minny, be drawn near to her. Wanted her focus, her concentration. Wanted her to reach forward with light fingers and gently caress—

"You're still here."

Henry drew himself up. "I am not going anywhere."

"In that case, you're going to get very hot and watch a woman work very hard," said Minny lightly. "I would have thought a man like you would have better things to do. Like earn a living of your own."

The Duchy of Dulverton had an annual income of twenty thousand pounds a year. Henry had worked hard to increase it, though his father had left the estate in a reasonably good sense of repair, and he was hopeful that some investments into cotton, a fabric one kept hearing praised, would eventually show dividends.

"Yes," he said uncertainly. "A living."

Minny turned away to pick up a hammer, one a little larger than the one she had thrust in his general direction yesterday. Henry watched as she laid the sickle in the flames, her hands moving swiftly around the metal.

There was something rather intoxicating about watching someone at work who truly knew what they were doing. Henry had discovered this while fencing. The way a person who was absolutely convinced of their own superiority—and could back it up with action—moved through space was mesmerizing.

Minny Banfield had the exact same manner as old Chantmarle. Without looking at him, as though he had disappeared from the world, she waited until a particular moment in time that looked to Henry just like any other.

Then she swiftly removed the sickle from the fire, placed it on the anvil, and lifted the hammer over her head.

Clang!

The noise reverberated around Henry's mind as well as the forge as he watched in amazement at the skill of the woman before him.

Clang!

Every hit, every tap was considered. Minny's eyes were narrowed as she focused entirely on the task before her, knocking out nicks too small for Henry's eyes to see.

"The trouble is," she said in a low voice under the clatter and clanging of her craft, "I have a village full of these, and horse shoes, and the plough, and nails—and no time for teaching."

In a sudden rush, she lifted the sickle and plunged it into the water in a butt beside her. The hissing and spluttering continued for a good while as she looked up, forehead puckered and eyes bright.

Henry swallowed. *Dear God, she was magnificent.* "I can pay you. Lots."

It was the wrong thing to say.

Suspicion crowded the previously unadulterated joy that had suffused Minny's face. "Yes, you mentioned money yesterday. Why? What do you want—and how does a man like you have money to waste, anyway?"

They were excellent questions, ones that in any other circumstance, Henry would have been unable to answer.

But he had seen the gleam in her eyes. Had seen it yesterday and saw it again today as he mentioned the money he was willing to give her for her time and expertise.

Here was a woman, Henry reasoned, who needed money. Who could not turn down money offered with very little effort. Who would consider him a fool for offering it, but a rich fool.

A rich fool was easily taken advantage of in London. Surely Pathstow could not be much different.

Minny lifted the sickle and examined it closely, using it as a distraction while she thought.

Henry's breath caught in his throat as he tried to force his lungs to move as he waited.

It was because of Peggy, he told himself, *that this mattered so much. Because of his sister.*

Certainly not because leaving Miss Minny Banfield's presence was starting to feel like a punishment, one he dearly would avoid at all costs.

He had to find the proof of her passing information to the newspaper.

"How long do you want to learn for?" she asked slowly, lowering the sickle onto the anvil.

A spark of hope rushed through Henry's chest. "Weeks. A few months maybe, at the most. I will then have to return to my...family."

Minny's gaze was sharp as it looked him up and down. "They don't mind being without you for that time?"

Henry tried not to think about the note he had left with Mrs. Coolidge, their housekeeper. Pegs would have read it by now and would surely expect him to reappear soon enough to accompany her to her next invitation. She may even go alone. Even though it would mean she would surely receive the cut from anyone in the *ton*.

Until he proved these scandalous rumors false, his sister would have to suffer that indignity. That was why he was here.

Outrageously pretty blacksmiths, notwithstanding.

"They will understand," Henry said, hoping rather than believing his statement to be true. "So, you will teach me, then?"

The decision warred in her eyes, bright and shining in the glow of the furnace, but Henry saw her shoulders slump in defeat before she spoke. He had won.

"Fine," Minny said darkly. "But don't say I didn't warn you."

CHAPTER FOUR

April 2, 1810

A S MINNY FINISHED her breakfast—nothing special, just some eggs Ted's daughter had brought round as a thank you for completing the sickles for her husband so swiftly—her mind started to wander.

Would he come?

It all felt like a dream after waking in the cold bedchamber above the forge.

"So you will teach me, then?"

"Fine. But don't say I didn't warn you."

Had she really said that? Would Mr. Everleigh really come?

More importantly, Minny thought as she washed her plate and the frying pan in the bucket of water at the back door, *would he pay her?*

For that was the only reason she was even thinking of permitting this. There could be no other reason; he was an insensitive, brutish, idiotic—

"So, where do we begin?"

Minny whirled around, wiping her damp hands on her gown as she stared at Mr. Everleigh.

He was leaning against the doorframe with a wry smile, as though congratulating himself for having discovered her. *In a most irritating fashion,* Minny decided, ignoring the pattering of her heart that threatened to tell quite a different story.

It was most unusual for a man to come around the back of the house, and Minny hated how the unexpected appearance of the man so unsettled her. It was most provoking.

Still. She was not about to be utterly stunned by a mere man. Even if his eyes sparkled.

"You're here then," she said stiffly. "Finally."

Mr. Everleigh's confidence immediately started to wane. "I had not realized you had expected me earli—"

"When one is a blacksmith, Mr. Everleigh, one has to learn to be up and about earlier than everyone else," Minny said sharply, turning away.

She did so in an attempt to demonstrate just how little she cared about his presence. This was, after all, her kitchen. Her home.

The trouble was, it had the unintended effect of making her unsure whether he was looking at her. *Of course he was looking.* She could feel the heat of his gaze on the back of her neck, hotter than any furnace.

Minny wished to goodness her neck wasn't pinking, as she was sure it was.

Then she wished she had not turned around—but she could not immediately whirl back, could she?

Trying to distract herself, she picked up a tea towel, shook it out, then started to fold it again. "I shall expect you here the moment day breaks."

"Whatever you want of me, Miss Banfield," came the low, teasing reply.

Minny's stomach lurched. *Oh, that such a voice could speak to her...almost as intimate as a lover's.* Not that she had much experience...

She turned around. Mr. Everleigh was smiling, but his expression soon fell.

"Now, you will find outside that door a large pile of logs that need quartering."

Mr. Everleigh drew back and glanced to his left. "So there is."

"And an ax."

Minny almost laughed aloud as the man's eyes widened. *Well, he had not expected special treatment, surely?* A man like him could not just turn up at a forge and act the gift horse and not expect her to take advantage.

"You cannot mean me to—"

"Welcome to the beginning of your training, Mr. Everleigh," Minny said smartly, placing the tea towel down and folding her arms as she grinned. "One of the most important tasks in a forge is to keep the furnace blazing. That is what you will be helping me with."

She watched, eagerly taking in every twist of expression on the man's face as he clearly tried to compose himself.

Not on your high horse now, are you?

"But I thought—at the very least I would be with you in the forge!"

Minny raised an eyebrow. "You did, did you?"

Her mother had warned her about men. Men who would expect things, try to take what wasn't theirs. No man had been foolish enough to try it, not yet, but Minny was prepared.

And if Mr. Everleigh had cooked up this whole charade in an attempt to be alone with her by the anvil—

"Miss Banfield," he started, taking a step forward.

Minny's smile immediately disappeared. "Did I give you permission to come into my home?"

Her icy tones could not have told him more swiftly how unwelcome he was. Her heart had also, rather painfully, skipped a beat as he did so. It refused to settle into a calming pattern as he stepped back.

"My apologies, I did not—"

"You seem to be under the mistaken impression that I want you here, Mr. Everleigh," said Minny quietly, fixing her gaze on the man. "You have convinced me, yes, but I am yet to see any money, or any reason why I should give you any knowledge of my craft. Now pay up, and get chopping."

Oh, it was exhilarating to be able to speak to a man like this! Minny tilted her head proudly, boldly, enjoying the way Mr. Everleigh just had to stand there and listen to her!

Would she ever have the opportunity to speak like this to a man again? Perhaps never.

Mr. Everleigh thrust a hand into a pocket and pulled out something that glittered. "Here."

Minny hesitated, then reached out. It would be churlish to expect him to throw it into the room after she had all but forbidden him from entering.

Their fingers touched as the guinea was transferred from one to another, and she tried not to gasp at the intense heat between them. *Dear God, it was hotter than the forge!* It was her imagination, surely— but her imagination had never given her such blazing warmth, such intensity of—

"All the wood?" Mr. Everleigh asked wearily.

Minny blinked, attempting to center herself after such an encounter. *He had not felt it too, then?*

She forced herself to nod curtly. "All the wood."

Turning, Minny left the kitchen and entered the forge. She closed the door behind her and leaned against it. *She had more than enough danger in her life at the moment, did she not?*

So why was she risking it all by having a man like that—a man who just with one simple touch of his fingers could throw her heart into such paroxysms?

The sound of very poor chopping came through the open window. Then—

"Oh, blast!"

The heavy thudding sound of wood falling from a chopping block made Minny chuckle. Everyone thought chopping wood was easy, but there was a real knack to it.

The furnace was almost at the right temperature, her arms already aching from the bellows, when she heard it again. A thud as wood slipped from the chopping block, the heavy thump of an ax being dropped into grass.

"Damn and blast it!"

Minny snorted. It was no worse than she had heard her father say when burning his hand accidentally, or seeing a perfectly good piece of metal go to waste because someone was careless.

Still. She had no wish to lose all the wood. It would surely be destroyed if she did not go and rescue it.

Rescue him.

Sighing heavily, and wondering whether all this was worth a guinea—safely tucked away in the strongbox at the back of the forge along with the next note she had to pass along—Minny placed down the bellows, wiped her forehead, and meandered outside.

All around the chopping block was wood. Not carefully quartered logs, as she had hoped. Not even halved, which was all she could manage some days when her arms ached from pumping the bellows and her hands were heavy after delicate work at the anvil.

No. Mr. Everleigh was standing there, sweat beaded on his brow, jacket off, and sleeves rolled up over muscular arms, frustration clear in his eyes as he surveyed the broken, chipped, and whole logs.

Minny's gaze wandered where it absolutely should not. From his hands, still grasping the ax, to his forearms, scattered with dark hair and pulsing in rage. His upper arms, partially hidden by linen sleeves that could not hide the strength within them.

His chest, broad and heaving as he fought to catch his breath.

His eyes…

Minny gasped as their eyes met. *This was foolishness,* she told herself. She was merely seeing things that weren't there, that was all. Feeling things that weren't there.

She leaned against the doorframe, much as he had done earlier that morning. "Having fun?"

Contrary to her expectations, Mr. Everleigh was able to smile. "Not in the slightest. How does your man do this?"

Minny blinked. "My man?"

What had he heard? Surely the gossip could not have reached the village; but no, she could trust them all. They would not make tittle-tattle out of what they already knew to be the truth.

Especially not to a stranger. *They would not betray her.*

"Your manservant, whoever normally does this," Mr. Everleigh said with a wave of his hand toward the logs.

"Manservant?"

"You don't call him a manservant?"

A wry smile crept across Minny's face. "Let me show you."

She strode forward at once, hardly knowing what was propelling her save the fact that she knew precisely the expression she would cause on that handsome face. It was always pleasant to prove someone wrong.

Taking the ax from his unresisting hands and trying not to breathe in the heady scent of the man's efforts, Minny did not look at him as she pushed him away.

"Give me some room," she said airily, picking up one of the logs he had attempted to chop in two.

Placing it carefully on the chopping block—an old tree stump, one that had been there even when she was a child—Minny eyed it and aligned herself beside it.

Her fingers gripped, then relaxed, then gripped. Her shoulders settled. She swung.

Thump!

The log fell from the chopping block in two equally sized halves.

If she were not very much mistaken, the man behind her breathed a word that had to be a curse—only swearwords were spoken like that.

But it wasn't one she had heard before.

She would have to save that for future use.

"There," Minny said with a grin, turning back to Mr. Everleigh. "Easy as—oh."

Mr. Everleigh had been a lot closer than she had expected. So close, in fact, that when she turned around, she turned into his arms.

Arms that steadied her as her legs threatened to fold underneath her.

Minny looked into the stern and yet impressed look of the man she had somehow managed to claim as a strange sort of temporary apprentice. Her breath caught in her throat.

He was not supposed to be this close.

"Minny Banfield, you astonish me," Mr. Everleigh breathed, his dark eyes lingering on her lips before returning to her eyes. "How did you do that?"

Minny tried to swallow, tried to have enough breath in her lungs to speak. "I-I—"

"I thought you said you had a manservant to do that."

And it was the mention of the manservant that—finally—returned her to her senses. Minny was not about to betray her brother.

She shrugged her way out of the—it was not an embrace, but she did not know what to call it. Whatever it was, she released herself.

"I said no such thing, I think you will find, Mr. Everleigh," she said as coldly as she could manage. A great feat, considering how warm she felt, even in the early-April air. "You assumed I had a servant. A woman who cannot chop logs cannot hope to run a forge."

His gaze flickered to the smithy, then back to her. Minny managed to keep her head high.

She had nothing to be ashamed of. She spoke the truth. How would she have kept that blaze going if she had to wait around for a man to get to the wood?

"Henry."

Minny allowed the ax to slip, gently, from her fingers onto the ground. In truth, she was not sure she could carry it much longer. There was something about this man that undid her.

"I beg your pardon?" she said stiffly.

There was a dancing amusement in the man's eyes now that she did not like. "Henry. It's my name. I suggest you use it."

The very idea! "Mr. Everleigh is perfectly—"

"Formal, a footing I have no desire to be on with you," he interrupted with mischievous eyes. "Do not fear, I will not presume to call you…they call you Minny at the inn, Miss Banfield?"

Minny swallowed. *This was not the plan.* The plan was to exhaust the brute with chopping logs all day, for several days if required, until the idiot got bored and wandered off. Went back to London or wherever he came from. Returned to whatever foolishness he had left.

He wasn't supposed to be here, all charming and interesting—

Minny narrowed her eyes. "Miss Banfield will do."

"I would still like to call you—"

"I am sure you would," she said curtly, striding back toward the kitchen, to safety. *To safety? Now where had that thought come from?* "But I am afraid you will find, Mr. Everleigh, that I am in no mood for informality. If you cannot cut wood, then you can do this."

Minny picked up the large buckets and held them aloft.

Henry—*Mr. Everleigh, she must not get into bad habits*—stared. "Buckets?"

She sighed. *What on earth had this man done before he had come to darken her doorway? The man had never seen buckets before?*

"Yes, buckets," she said impatiently. The furnace would be almost cold now, all her hard work to get it ablaze wasted. And she had a pair of horseshoes to do and a plough to straighten. "Buckets. For water. From the well."

Henry continued to stare. Eventually, he said, "You cannot mean for me to—that's servant work!"

The words had escaped his mouth seemingly before he could stop them. Minny stared, curiosity curling around her heart.

Well, yes, of course it was. Or homesteader's work. Or the work of someone like her, who had no ability to pay for servants and so had to do the hard work oneself.

Something Mr. Everleigh should be entirely aware of...but the way that he said—

"I mean," Henry said hastily, correcting himself. "The work of your manservant."

"How many times do I have to tell you," Minny said testily, "I do not have—"

"No man at all about the place? No one coming here to help you, no brother, no friends...at all?"

Minny swallowed. Henry's face was all of a sudden sharp, questioning her as though there was a secret he could winkle out of her.

And she had one, more's the pity, Minny thought wretchedly. Not one she would give up lightly. No one would ever hear the truth from her lips. She had sworn, hadn't she? To keep it a secret. To protect those she loved, those who could not protect themselves.

And no man, not even a handsome one, was going to make her give up her brother.

"I heard tell at the King's Head a man comes to help you on occasion," Henry persisted.

"The well is on the village green," she said quietly, refusing to rise to the bait.

For a moment, they stood there, the buckets between them, locked in a strange battle of wills Minny did not understand. Yes, it was possible Ted could have mentioned her brother. He would not think of the danger. It was natural village chatter, hardly even gossip, to mention her brother's infrequent visits.

Minny tried not to show the fear warring in her heart.

But that did not mean she was going to explain anything. No one would understand, particularly not a stranger.

"The village green," Henry said eventually.

Minny tried to smile. "I am sure you'll find your own way back."

"I certainly will."

It was a relief to return to the prickling heat of the forge. Minny breathed out slowly as she pressed her hands to the cooling anvil.

How was it possible for a man she had met but days ago to get so swiftly under her skin? Why was it so easy for him to irritate her?

Minny closed her eyes for a moment, grounding herself on the anvil, the part of her life that would never change, never alter.

The forge, the furnace, the anvil, the tools of her trade. They were what she could count on. They were her livelihood.

And so, for the rest of the day, Minny did just that. She made two horse shoes and sent them over to Farmer Jones with a note saying she could fit them herself, if he wished. She undertook the complex mending of the plough, bent after hoeing a line over an old oak tree whose roots had crept toward the sky. She made a note in the pocketbook of the work, and the charges, and who had paid and who had not.

She mended two of her own hammers, which had become slightly unbalanced. She made a note of how much wood she would need brought in and whether there was sufficient iron for the rest of the month.

And Minny studiously did not watch Henry Everleigh.

She did not watch him walk along the road, through the small forge window, to the well. She did not watch him strain against the well rope, his strength visible even from a distance. She did not watch him return, time and time again, with heavy buckets slopping water as he filled the trough at the back of the forge.

She especially did not watch him slyly from the kitchen window as she went to make herself a small luncheon platter, attempting to chop the logs again. His determination to prove himself was delightful, as was the way he learned, slowly, his arms clearly aching by the end of the afternoon.

Minny sighed as she wiped her hands on a cloth as the day neared its end. She could not lie to herself.

Every minute of the entire day, she had been conscious of where Henry Everleigh was. With each passing hour, her curiosity grew.

He was a strong man, even if he had seemingly never done some of the most basic chores a body could do. So where had he come from? What did he truly want with her, with her forge?

It was a mercy he had not asked to sleep at the forge. Minny started to hang up her tools, clean and ready for work the next day. The thought of Henry in the bedchamber next to hers—

"Miss Banfield?"

Minny almost dropped the hammer. "What?"

She whirled around and saw much to her irritation that Henry— that Mr. Everleigh was smiling.

"I thought I would let you know that I am going back to the King's Head now," he said calmly. "I hope my work has pleased you."

The highly suggestive word made Minny blanch. "I am sure I—Mr. Everleigh, where do you come from?"

The smile immediately disappeared. "What business is that of yours?"

Ah, now that was interesting. "Only that if trouble were to come to my forge, I would be responsible for you as your employer," Minny said as matter-of-factly as she could manage. "I have the right, I think, to know a little of your history."

Now that was interesting. As curious as the man was, it appeared he was in no mood to reveal anything about himself. That was, if the tight-lipped, cold expression was anything to go by.

"My history is dull," he said quietly. "I have worked hard all my life in my father's…business. I have left that business behind. For now."

Minny hesitated. There was evidently scandal there, but then, who has not wished to leave behind one's life at times and start out afresh? Was she to judge a man merely because he had managed it?

"I pay you to learn your craft," said Henry quietly. "Not reveal anything about myself—and as we are on the topic of your craft, when will I have the opportunity to—"

"Not today," Minny said heavily.

The very thought of picking up a hammer now...no. Her bones were tired and her mind ached with the intensity of Henry's presence. She needed to be alone.

"Tomorrow?"

Her eyes met the determined gaze of the man before her, and Minny's treacherous heart fluttered. *He really was most attractive.*

"Perhaps."

CHAPTER FIVE

April 4, 1810

H ENRY BLEW OUT a long, exhausted breath, and tried not to let his shoulders slump.

Dear God, he had never worked so hard. Well, that was not precisely true. His father had forced him to be involved in the running of the estates from a young age. He'd looked over more ledgers by the time he reached one and twenty than most people saw in a lifetime.

But that was different. Not like—

"Ah, you are finished," said Miss Banfield brightly, her sleeves rolled up and her leather apron most irritatingly hiding her curves. "Excellent, I have another job for you."

Henry could not help it. He groaned.

"Please, I beg you," he said, losing all sense of dignity in his attempt to gain rest. "Just five minutes. I just need to sit for—"

"I thought you wanted to truly understand what it was like to be a blacksmith?" asked Miss Banfield, eyebrow raised and a teasing smile on her beautiful face. "Have you seen me sit yet today?"

Henry leaned against the wall in the forge, sweltering from the exertions he had been put to combined with the intense heat coming from the furnace, and tried not to think of Miss Banfield sitting. Sitting in his lap. Sitting on his—

"No, you have not," she said tartly, laying down a hammer on the anvil and putting her hands on her hips. "You wanted to learn. Some of the best lessons are hard won."

If Henry had any energy left in his body, he would have replied. But he was exhausted.

Three days. How had it only been three days?

It was bad enough being forced to eat food at the King's Head—nothing to what his cook at Dulverton Manor could produce—and sleep in a bed not fit for a dog.

But his hands!

Henry curled his hands behind his back as he accepted the steady gaze of the woman before him. His hands ached. No, it was worse than that. They were blistered, calloused, crying out for relief, but he had given them no quarter.

After the humiliating display Miss Banfield had given him—he was certain chopping wood was far more difficult than that—he had never sought sympathy nor permitted a complaint to pass his lips.

Well. Except for just now.

Miss Banfield shook her head. "There are many who think being a blacksmith is all hitting things in the warmth, but there's a great deal of work behind it."

Henry could do nothing but nod, head weary, shoulders aching.

This was no life for a duke!

But he wasn't a duke here, was he? It was starting to become second nature. Changing his speech, ensuring the flowery language expected of a gentleman addressed as "Your Grace" was gone. Changing the way he stood, all elegance removed.

That wasn't hard. His back would never be the same again after carrying all that water.

And worst of all…he'd spent all that time outside, while Miss Banfield was inside. Away from his gaze.

"Well, if you are truly tired," said Miss Banfield genially, as though she was giving him a favor. "You may rest for a few minutes and…and watch me work. If you would like."

Her eyes met his. Henry was delighted to see a flush tinge her cheeks. *Now, that was interesting.*

Being around Miss Banfield had arguably been more difficult than the tasks she had set him. She was intoxicating, a heady medley of independence and boldness, brashness yet shyness.

There was something about her that drew him—that would surely draw any thinking man. Or unthinking man, if it came to it.

But she had never given any sign of wishing to draw his attention, much less his attraction. Until now.

Hunger for her rose in his chest. Henry examined her, the delicate figure that surely hid muscles earned through hard work. The faint smile that sometimes trespassed her lips, the way her eyes—

"So you can learn," Miss Banfield said, most unfairly interrupting his thoughts. "Mr. Everleigh, are you listening to me?"

Henry swallowed. It was most unfortunate that he could not lose himself in a few more minutes of just looking, appreciating the form that was Miss Banfield.

A man could only struggle against such appreciation for so long.

But she was alone here, and unprotected, he reminded himself. He was a gentleman.

And, far more importantly, she was part of the gossip network, Henry tried to remember. She was the reason Peg was no longer welcome in so many drawing rooms. This Miss Banfield, though she may look innocent, was a traitor to her kind, and surely benefitting from it financially to boot.

"Mr. Everleigh?"

Henry cleared his throat. "My name, as I have said before, is Henry."

As their eyes met, a rush of warmth soared through him—but apparently, not her. Miss Banfield turned nonchalantly to pick up a fine tool from the bench behind her.

"I am well aware of that."

Henry waited. By God, if she knew who he was…there was not a young lady in the whole of the *ton* who would not bite his hand off to speak on a first name basis.

But of course, Miss Banfield had no idea who he was. It was rather…well, freeing. Henry had never disliked being a duke. It was like disliking one's lungs or the sunshine around you. It was just there.

It was only now that he was starting to realize just what he lost by having such a title. The gentle familiarity of those around you. The freedom to speak. To think without censure.

"And I can call you…?" he persisted.

He knew her name was Minny, of course. Had already used it, though she had not appreciated that.

But calling her by her name…for some reason, Henry longed to. It was an intimacy that would put them on an even footing.

When Miss Banfield turned to him, placing the tool on the anvil, her face was still flushed—though of course that could be because of the heat of the place. His face was certainly as flushed.

But he could hope, could he not, it was his presence giving such roses to her cheeks?

"My name," she said slowly, not quite meeting his eyes. "You can call me Minny."

Henry stared. *God, he would be danger here if she were anything like his rank.* How did she manage to exude such delicious attraction yet appear so innocent, so unknowing? Why did she permit him here if his presence rattled her so?

The memory of the guinea he had handed over three days ago nudged him, but Henry pushed it aside.

Even for money, a woman would not allow a man to so intrude in her life if she had no wish for it.

So…so she wanted him here?

"Minny," he repeated.

By Jove, he would have to be careful. That was a powerful incentive to call out her name day and night—

"Mary, really," Minny said with a laugh, all tension gone. "But my mother was Mary, and so they called me Minny. M-I-N-N-Y."

"Minny," Henry said again.

It suited her. It was a delight to say. He could not put his finger on why, though the thought of putting his finger anywhere close to Minny made his stomach lurch.

"Yes, I suppose it is an odd name," she said. "My brother always said—"

And then the moment was over. Henry straightened up, moving away from the wall as he saw the cloud descend.

"My brother always said—"

Now there was a slip of the tongue and no mistake. Henry watched carefully for any clue on Minny's face, but all the walls which had been there when they had first met had returned.

Minny Banfield had no wish to speak of her brother.

A strange excitement sparked in Henry's chest. So, that was surely the man the owner of the King's Head had mentioned, the man seen infrequently but consistently returning to the forge. Never to stay long.

Just the sort of man who might be taking letters to London.

It was odd. Just for a moment, a few seconds as they had smiled at each other, Henry had forgotten why he was here in the first place. He had just been a man looking at a woman who attracted him, hoping she was as attracted as he felt.

But that was gone, over. He may not have seen any evidence of notes, of messages being passed, of strangers meeting here to take gossip to London...but he had only been here a few days.

Henry tried to force the emotions he was not going to name aside. He was here for Peg, for all the other ladies of Society who had suffered.

Not to seduce delightfully bold blacksmiths...

"You wanted to watch me," said Minny quietly, picking up her tool as though she had said nothing of a sibling.

Henry swallowed, knowing what he wanted to say and just how inappropriate it would be—but the words slipped past his lips before he could stop them. "I could watch you all day."

Yes, that was definitely a flush. Higher up, right in the apples of her cheeks.

A lurch in his stomach—or in truth, a little lower—confirmed she was not alone in feeling a little warm.

"R-Right," Minny said, evidently uncertain. "There's a stool there you can sit on."

Her gaze dropped immediately to the anvil, as though she could no longer bring herself to look at him.

Henry's chest tightened as he lowered himself gently onto the three legged stool.

If they had met in London, or Bath—or even Brighton, which was becoming more popular with each passing Season. Why, if they had met anywhere but over an anvil, he would have been delighted to discover just what an effect he could have on a pretty woman like her.

"Right," Minny muttered under her breath, ignoring Henry completely.

He would have been piqued, if it were not so interesting. There was a real art to blacksmithing, one could see in an instant. The expert eye the young woman cast over the object on the anvil—some sort of iron hook, as far as Henry could see. The confident way she thrust it into the furnace. The way she knew precisely how long to leave it there before returning it to the anvil.

The rhythmic taps she gave it echoed Henry's own rapidly increasing heartbeat.

Every inch of him was...well, more alive when in the smithy. Henry could not explain it. There was something so primal, so instinctive about the way Minny worked the metal.

Something so attractive about the way she seemed to know precisely when to put the iron hook back into the fire, when to bring it out, when to push the metal a little harder, when to soften the blows.

It was intoxicating.

Henry had never seen anything like it. The mastery she had over her craft was exhilarating.

Unable to help himself, Henry slowly rose from his stool. He hardly had the best position, after all, on a level with the anvil. If he wanted to see precisely what she was doing...

Minny did not look up. It were as though he was not there.

In any other situation, Henry would have been offended, but it was impossible to be so with such an intriguing woman before him. His chest tightened, his breathing ragged as he stepped closer.

The iron hook was almost mended. It was an intricate piece of work, something he would never have imagined could be possible with just a few small hammers.

He stepped closer.

"Careful."

Minny's word was quiet yet sharp, and Henry halted immediately in his steps.

Dear God, he was transfixed, hypnotized by her work. He had quite forgot himself: the reason he had come here, the interest he had in her...all faded away.

Both sensations returned with a vengeance. Henry glanced over, the perspiration on her brow, the concentration she paid the delicate work.

How could a woman like this, who so evidently had to work hard for a living, permit herself to be drawn in with such rogues? But then, wasn't that the problem? That she so desperately needed money?

"What's that?"

"My maker's mark," Minny said without looking at him.

Henry nodded sagely. "So everyone will know this is your craftsmanship."

She narrowed her eyes as she focused. "Of course. I want people to see my impressive work and know to come to me for the work."

"Can—Can I have a go?"

Henry had not intended to speak, but the desire to be closer Minny was too great. Perhaps if she could show him how to hit that small hammer just so, he could reach out and—

"It's too slight," Minny said, still not looking up.

Henry took another step forward, unable to help himself. He was right by the anvil now, the heat of the furnace growing. "But I want to learn."

"You'll learn when you're ready," Minny said quietly. "Move back, it's dangerous."

It was done in a moment. Henry reached forward just as she moved to return the iron hook to the furnace and—

"Ye gods!"

Henry snapped his arm back, wringing his hand as the scalding iron burned his wrist. Never having broken a bone nor experienced anything but a discomforting fall once from the kitchen garden wall, it was a new pain—a most unwelcome one.

"Henry Everleigh, what did I say!" Minny thrust down her work unceremoniously onto the anvil and stepped round in a swift movement. "Come here!"

Before Henry knew what she was doing, before he barely knew what he was doing, Minny had reached for him. She took his hand in hers, brought it swiftly up to her eyes to take a professional look, and—

Henry blinked.

She had placed her lips around the burn. Her tongue met his skin. Then she sucked.

It was all Henry could do not to collapse onto the floor. Oh, the hedonistic sensations flittering up his arm was more than he could bear. Minny stood there, her lips around the edge of his wrist, delicately licking and sucking, and his very toes were curling.

Dear God, he would have to bed her. He could do nothing else, this was the most intimate, the most—

Minny released her mouth from his wrist, then took another careful look. "There we go."

Henry tried to force his manhood down from attention, tried to remember this was a forge and it would be most unseemly for a duke to bed a woman here.

Not that he didn't want to.

"Y-You…you…" he stammered.

A flush was tinging Minny's cheeks again, but she had not released his hand. "It's the quickest way to calm a burn, th-that's all. I just—I would have done it for—"

And that was when Henry lost all control.

Would have done it for anyone?

No, that was the last thing he wanted to hear. He would not hear it. He would stop that mouth at once.

Henry crushed his lips upon hers, all the pent-up tension and desire he had fought since he had first clapped eyes on the woman pouring onto her mouth. His hand was still clasped in hers, but his free hand grasped at her waist, pulling her closer.

And instead of fighting him off, pushing him away, telling him in no uncertain terms she had no wish to be taken advantage of…

Minny sank into his kiss.

Henry moaned, unable to help himself. She was sweet and warm, yet there was a fire in her he had never expected. Not fire—passion. She met his own desire with something powerful of her own, leaning into his arms and parting her lips to welcome him in.

Welcome the heady appetite he certainly should not be permitting.

Hating himself for kissing her, and hating himself even more for ending what promised to be a superb kiss, Henry regretfully released the blacksmith and pulled back.

Minny's hair was mussed, her lips dark pink from the strength of his ardor, and unless Henry was very much mistaken, he was in a similar state.

"Ah," he said aloud, unhelpfully.

Oh, hell's bells. This was not the intention, though it made him wonder why he had not considered this in the first place. All this chopping wood and carrying water business could have been replaced with a simple seduction.

A bedding—pleasurable to them both—then pillow talk, in which he would have discovered everything that he needed to know. But now...

"Oh," said Minny, eyes downcast.

Henry swallowed. *Hell, this was not the plan.* The plan was to find out where the devil this gossip was coming from, not to kiss unmarried, unprotected, and surely strong enough to beat him in a pinch, young ladies.

"I-I should not have kissed—"

"I shouldn't have—your wrist—"

They spoke together, awkward words mingling. Tension pulled Henry's shoulders taut as his instinct—to leave immediately—warred against his better judgment.

He could not just ignore this. He was determined to stay, learn blacksmithing, and root out whether Minny Banfield was the source of his sister's downfall.

And that was all. *And that meant that somehow,* Henry thought wretchedly, *he would have to fix this.*

"I apologize," he said stiffly, taking another step back. *When had this forge become so damned small?*

Minny glanced up. "You apologize? For what?"

Why did the woman have to be so...so obstinate! "For kissing you."

Henry had never expected to feel so unbalanced in the presence of a woman.

She had raised an eyebrow. "I would have thought you'd be apologizing for the real error."

He stared. *Error?* God, what had he done now? Was there some sort of blacksmith code that prevented a man from—

"Reaching out like that taught you a...a lesson, I suppose," Minny said, nodding meaningfully at his wrist.

Her quick thinking had reduced the burn to a mere red mark, but it still stung like blazes. He hadn't noticed with Minny in his arms.

His stomach lurched. Not a good enough reason to pull her back into them.

"Right," he said aloud. "Yes. I am sorry, Minny."

Their eyes met, and he saw something there he had not expected. Hurt. Pain, unlike that currently throbbing his wrist. No, there was something else; pain he had apologized for the kiss?

"I think that's probably enough work for one day," she said quietly.

Henry nodded. *Yes, he'd had enough: enough intoxicating pleasure, enough temptation.* But he couldn't stay away, couldn't bring himself to leave her. Not yet.

"I would like to see you finish the iron hook, if that is acceptable," he said quietly, lowering himself on the stool and praying his legs would be stronger by the time he rose again. "If you will permit me to stay and watch."

Her hesitation was not unwarranted, but Henry hoped with every fiber of his being—

"Fine," Minny said. "As long as you can promise to keep your hands off me."

Henry smiled weakly. "I make no promises."

CHAPTER SIX

April 8, 1810

MINNY LET OUT a long, slow, and careful breath as her eyes flickered across the page.

Had she included everything? She could not recall any additional information Alan had requested, and she had tried to fit as much into the cramped handwriting as possible. True, there were a few smudges, but her brother was accustomed to deciphering her truly atrocious spelling.

It was a marvel the two of them could both read and write, she thought wistfully as she carefully folded the paper once, twice, a third time. If it hadn't been for their mother's insistence, this whole operation would have been impossible.

As it were...

Minny carefully cut a length of brown string with her knife and tied it securely around the letter. A richer person would have perhaps sealed it with wax, but she couldn't spend the few pennies she had on such a luxury.

The kitchen was empty, the early morning light just starting to drift through the windows as Minny opened the back door. She glanced around. No one was about, that was one of the few benefits of this time of year. In the summer, she had to rise obscenely early to hide the notes in time, before the farmers and other villagers were up and about.

Carefully, she wedged the letter behind the trough.

Then, and only then, did she slowly allow her shoulders to loosen.

There. Done, for another week. It had been a worry the last few days trying to think how she would achieve such a thing with Henry—with Mr. Everleigh so frequently in the forge.

But it was done. When her brother slipped by at night, he would find precisely what he was expecting.

"Good morning, Minny."

A few days ago, Minny might have jumped. Her heart might have quickened from the surprise; she might have whirled around hastily to see who had spoken.

But she didn't now.

At least, her heartbeat had quickened, but not from the surprise. No, from the delight.

Minny tried to force it away as she nodded politely. "Mr. Everleigh."

It had been a mistake to permit the nickname her family had given her. She knew her cheeks flushed at the sound of her name on his lips. If only he wasn't so expert with those lips.

He was grinning. Minny tried to smile back as she simultaneously tried not to think about the kiss they had shared a few days ago.

A kiss! It was a marvel she was able to consider it so dispassionately as she turned away from the handsome man who had trespassed so inconveniently on her dreams last night.

When a woman received her first kiss, and from such a handsome man, in the privacy of her own forge, she was sure no one else would consider it just "a kiss."

Minny swallowed to ensure her voice was strong before she said, "And how are you this morning, Mr. Everleigh?"

Henry grinned as he leaned in the doorway of her kitchen. He knew better than to step inside it without an invitation.

There were some parts of her life, Minny thought darkly, *she really must try to keep for herself.* Her kitchen. The upstairs over the forge. Her heart.

Her brother…

"Oh, I slept very well, thank you, Minny," said Henry happily, evidently not noticing her frantic breathing. "In fact, I stepped out early with the sunrise and thought I would have a little wander around the village. And some very interesting things I saw, too."

Minny's heart skipped a beat as dread poured into her chest.

Surely…surely, she had not been so lax as to miss Henry Everleigh when she had stepped out to the trough?

Surely she had not betrayed—

"Really?" she said as calmly as she could manage.

It was such a shame his grin was so delightful. "Really."

She had to stay calm, that was all, Minny told herself. She had not just betrayed her brother. She had not—

"So, may I have my first lesson?"

Minny turned to see a hopeful expression on the tall man's face, and her lips quirked into a smile. It was rather delicious to have someone like Henry Everleigh in the palm of her hand. He wanted something she had—*not her kisses,* she told herself furiously. Her skills.

She wasn't sure which was better.

"I don't know," Minny said, smile broadening. Oh, it was so delightful to tease this man. It was a habit they had fallen into so swiftly. With anyone else it would have been scandalous. With him, of course, it was just a bit of fun. There was nothing serious in it.

She didn't dream wistfully of another one of those scalding kisses…

Henry groaned. "Minny Banfield, if you make me chop wood for another day—"

"You are at least getting slightly better," she pointed out, heart singing. "And you know how to draw water from a well now without pulling your shoulder."

He raised a finger. "That was something you should have told me the very first day."

Minny laughed, and he laughed with her, and she knew it was ridiculous to see something that wasn't there. Couldn't be there.

He's only here because you need the money, she tried to tell herself, most unsuccessfully. A guinea! He could stay all month for a guinea.

All month, all spring, into the autumn…

"So, have I proved myself worthy?" teased Henry, tilting his head. "Will you teach me?"

Minny hesitated, biting her lip. Only then did she realize Henry's eyes had drifted to her lips and were now strangely unfocused.

Her stomach turned. She was not here to seduce a man! She would not have her reputation, such as it was, ruined just because a man turned up at her forge, asked to be taught blacksmithing, and kissed like the devil.

"Fine," she said quickly, turning and stepping out of the kitchen and into the forge.

Anything to get away from that quizzical expression…it was almost as though he knew precisely what effect he was having on her.

And that would certainly not do.

"Fine?" came the astonished reply behind her. Henry followed her into the forge, the furnace not yet lit.

"Yes, fine."

"Y-You mean you'll teach me?"

If she were not mistaken, there was incredulity in the man's voice. "Well, why not?"

It was what she had asked herself mere moments ago, and Minny had been most disgruntled to discover she had no good answer.

After all, he had chopped wood, fetched water, mended that window. Minny had been astonished to find herself ordering him to take messages about the village—the nerve!—and even more astonished when he had obeyed.

That had required an awkward conversation with Farmer Jones, who had politely inquired when she had acquired a servant. On her own. In the forge.

That had been an error.

But there was only so much polishing a man could do, Minny thought with a repressed grin, before she had to admit he had done all the dull chores she hated, and without much complaining.

Even if he drew water all wrong.

"Goodness," Henry said with a dry laugh. "I did not think you would teach me."

Minny shot him a look. "I said I would, did I not?"

"You did, you did indeed," he said hastily.

It was difficult not to smile at his immediate change of direction. Well, it was pleasant to have a man about the place who would acquiesce to her opinion.

And he wasn't bad to look at, either.

"Minny?"

"What?" Minny said hastily, her gaze sharpening to find Henry looking at her most perplexed. *Goodness, she had entirely lost all concentration there!*

"You were going to teach me something," he said. "Until you were somehow otherwise occupied."

Minny glared. *Well, it was his own fault, wasn't it?* When Henry Everleigh had first appeared at her forge, he had been wearing a shirt, waistcoat, jacket, and overcoat. Most appropriately dressed.

For the outdoors in spring, that was. In a forge, one swiftly learned what not to wear to ensure one did not collapse from the heat. Minny could not recall the last time she had worn a petticoat, and as for stays and a corset!

No, her leather apron was the protection she needed.

But that did mean the handsome man had grown accustomed to

walking around in nothing but breeches, a shirt with sleeves rolled up, and a waistcoat.

A tightly fitted waistcoat that showed off the breadth and strength of his chest. Rolled up sleeves that revealed strong arms dusted in dark hair and a slight red mark still by his right wrist.

Minny swallowed. *She was not going to permit herself to be completely distracted in her own forge!*

"Right," she said mainly to herself. "Right, lesson one…"

Well, the whole thing was a farce, wasn't it? He couldn't really wish to be a blacksmith. He was too old to learn the profession and had to return to his family, as he said. Her stomach lurched. Perhaps a wife.

But that was not her concern. Minny may not understand why he was here, but she could give him an understanding of the basics.

He had paid her, after all.

Minny's gaze sharpened, and she placed her hands on the anvil. "Right. First of all we'll need to…"

Her voice trailed away. She had caught Henry staring as though…well, as though he was attracted to her.

There was no other way to describe it. A shot of heat, of excitement, of something akin to joy burned through Minny as she looked at him. Looked at him looking at her.

The fire hadn't been lit in the furnace, so there was no other explanation for why heat was rising steadily up her body. No other reason, except…

"Tools," Minny said hastily, turning from the temptation and placing her hands on the cool tools racked on the wall.

Not for the first time, the cool metal calmed her frantic heart, helping to slow her breathing as she took back control.

She was not going to make a fool of herself…at least, not any more of a fool than she already had been. Minny tried not to think of how she had immediately acquiesced to the kiss Henry had most unaccountably placed on her lips. The way that her hand had reached up to his lapel, bringing him closer…

"Yes, I have noticed you have a great number of different tools," came Henry's voice.

Minny nodded. That was it; all she had to do was talk about the tools. That was all.

Hammers, some far heavier than others for the really difficult work. Chisels for that delicate precision work that required a steady hand. The three sets she had, larger chisels with wooden handles for when the work got too hot. A hardy, Minny's most used chisel that fitted into the anvil—

"Yes, I saw you use that the day I met you."

Minny swallowed, heat rising through her chest. Why did such an innocuous sentence have to sound so…so intimate?

"Yes, I saw you use that the day I met you."

The day they met. Was it truly over a week ago? It seemed impossible. He was already such a feature of the forge, Minny hardly knew what she would do with herself when he left.

She would have to chop more logs, for a start.

"Yes, when I was mending a belt buckle," Minny said, focusing on the tool in her hand and not the handsome man looking carefully at it.

Her fingers curled around the instrument. It was cool to the touch, far cooler than her skin, which seemed to be rising in temperature with every passing moment.

"And then there's the forge itself, the bellows, the vent…" Minny found everything was easier if she just allowed her mouth to take over.

If she was talking about the forge, then she couldn't be asking the questions that dwelled in her heart.

What was he doing here? What did he really want?

And when he had what he wanted, whatever it was…he would leave, wouldn't he?

"And the anvil," Henry supplied, placing his hands upon it.

Minny placed the tool back on the rack and placed her own hands on the anvil with a grin. "My father's anvil. His father's anvil. The Banfield anvil."

His hands were just inches away. The cooling metal of the anvil seemed to have no impact on her feverishly warm skin.

Minny swallowed. This had all felt very innocent—in the company of another, perhaps it would be. But there was something intensely different about this conversation when with Henry.

"This is all so interesting," he said, enthused.

She raised an eyebrow. No one had ever described the smithy as interesting—certainly not with that tone.

Why, Alan had left as soon as he was able, only returning when he had run out of money or sense or both.

But Henry Everleigh…she did not know him well, of course. A mere matter of days.

Surely no one could falsify that look of genuine curiosity?

"I suppose it is," Minny confessed. "I have never thought about it like that. I have always…well. I enjoy it, of course. It's my life."

"Your livelihood," Henry nodded.

"My life." It was easy to correct him, easy to slip into this happy comfort Minny had somehow found with this man who had been a stranger to her just two weeks ago. "When one has little else, something like a forge can swiftly absorb one. Become everything one has, everything one knows."

Where had these words come from? Buried deep in her heart. Minny had never brought these sensations out into the light…but something about Henry drew them out.

It was most unaccountable.

"How did you find yourself here, alone?" Henry's voice was quiet, gentle, but he was so close, Minny could feel his breath on her neck. "You said this is the Banfield anvil?"

Yes, that was what she should cling to, Minny told herself. The story of her family, facts, history.

Not the soaring excitement she felt whenever Henry was in the room with her.

"This place has been the Banfield forge for generations," Minny said, forcing herself to step away from the anvil. *She could do it, any time she wanted. So why not now?* "My father was the blacksmith here for near on five and twenty years, and his father for a similar time before him."

"And before that?"

Minny grinned as she ran her hands over the tools. "The family legend is that the village grew up around the smithy, though I am not sure that can be taken as gospel."

He chuckled. "My father was similar, he always said…"

She watched as the light drifted from Henry's eyes, all excitement gone. *Interesting.*

"You mentioned, I think, a family business."

Henry nodded. "Yes, one I inherited—much like you inherited the forge, I suppose. Though did not your brother have a stronger claim?"

Minny's insides became ice. *This was the trouble*, she told herself fiercely, *of allowing your tongue to run away.* She had known Henry had picked up on that slip about her brother, and he was not going to let it lie.

The important thing was to act as though it did not matter. As though one's brother was just another part of the scenery. As though one did not fear for his life at every turn.

"Oh, my brother would have made a poor blacksmith," Minny said as airily as she could manage.

Evidently not enough.

"Really? I would have assumed…well, forgive me," said Henry with a dry laugh. "I know you can chop wood, and I am certain you can draw water. You forge well. But I would have thought this was a difficult life for a lady."

Minny had to laugh. "Me, a lady?"

"You know what I mean," said Henry, a teasing grin on his lips. "A woman."

She shrugged, though her pride was knocked. "I can smithy as well as any man."

"I did not say that you could not."

"Besides, I like having my own forge," Minny said, truth escaping before she could stop it. "How many women wish for their independence, their own choices, the opportunity to make a life for themselves?"

Henry blinked. "You...you know, I have never given it much thought."

Minny rolled her eyes. "So few men do. But if you had a sister, say, she may not wish to merely marry and bear children and keep house. She may have—oh, I don't know. Dreams of her own. Hopes. Ambitions, perhaps, a desire to earn great heaps of money."

Henry snorted. "Peggy would never dream of—I mean...well. I don't know, I suppose."

Minny smiled. Poor Peggy. She evidently had a well-meaning brother, but perhaps when he returned to wherever he came from, there would be a little more thought given to her future.

If she weren't married off already.

"It must be lonely."

Minny stiffened. There had been such...well, such care in Henry's voice. She glanced over at the tall man who was watching her with an unreadable expression.

"Nonsense," she said curtly. "I see half the village month in and month out, for one thing or another."

"It's not the same, and you know it."

Minny swallowed. She did know it. Sometimes she cried out in the night for the loneliness, aching for a lover's touch, but also the comfort of a friend in dark times, someone to laugh with during the good.

Not that she was about to admit to such a thing. "I get by."

"But you're alone," Henry persisted gently.

Minny met his gaze. "Not now."

The moment hung between them, aching with possibility. Minny knew if she launched herself toward him now, he would kiss her. He wouldn't be able to help himself; she knew attraction when she saw it, and he wanted kisses from her. Wanted more.

And she was smiling. *Dear God, was she...flirting?*

"And I think that's quite enough new knowledge for you," Minny said hastily, frowning as her smile disappeared. "I have a package you can deliver to the King's Head, a set of five saucepans for the cook."

Henry groaned.

"And I want you to be quick about it," Minny lied, desperate for a moment to herself to recover. "I'll have plenty of work for you when you get back."

Henry's eyes lit up. "Can I have a go at bashing something?"

Minny winched. "If you mean logs, absolutely."

CHAPTER SEVEN

April 12, 1810

I T REALLY WAS the strangest thing. The first night Henry had walked—more accurately, collapsed—back to the King's Head, he had lain on the small bed for at least an hour.

Partly from exhaustion. But partly because he had been forced to argue with himself, completely silently, about returning to the Banfield forge the next morning.

It simply had not felt worth it. Everything within him ached, his hands hurt, and Miss Banfield had most decidedly embarrassed him.

"Give me some room."

"Minny Banfield, you astonish me. How did you do that?"

And the enterprise did not appear to be getting him any closer to discovering whether she was part of the secret chain of gossip. Lies. Scandal.

Which was why Henry felt a bit of a fool. Because today, just a week later—no, was it more than a week?—he could hardly prevent a smile creeping up his lips as he descended the stairs into the King's Head dining area.

He would see her soon. Just a few minutes, then—

"Ah, someone's got a spring in their step," said Ted with a nod.

Henry tried not to smile. As though he could stop himself. As though the thought of being closer to Minny could in any way be extinguished.

It was maddening. All these social niceties, all keeping him from—

"Minny working you hard?"

Henry answered honestly. "Harder than I have ever worked in my life."

The older man nodded appreciatively. "Yes, it's a hard life, working in a forge. We all thought she would give it up, see. After her father died."

Henry nodded and hesitated by the door. Yes, he wished to see Minny again swiftly—precisely why, he could not admit to himself. Not yet.

But he could not miss this opportunity to learn more about her...about her family. About this brother she evidently had no wish to speak of.

"It must have been difficult. Taking on such a responsibility."

Ted nodded sagely. "Ah, she knew what she was doing alright, o'course, old Banfield taught her well. But it's different, isn't it, a woman being out there on her own."

Henry swallowed. The thought had occurred to him when he had realized, just yesterday, that Minny slept over the forge on her own.

It should not have come as a great surprise. It was not as though he had seen any servants, companions, even visitors beyond customers. It was clear she was alone.

But the idea of Minny being unprotected...

It had been all Henry could do to force himself to return to the King's Head that night.

"But there was a brother, I thought," Henry said, gently prodding the older man in the hope of additional information.

Information he received, though not through words. Ted's face darkened, a scowl crinkling his forehead, and he spat onto the floor.

"We don't speak of 'im," he said darkly before nodding his head.

"Good day, sir."

And that was that. Henry was not so blind as to ignore the obvious dismissal. He nodded and stepped out of the warm pub into the brisk early morning air.

He breathed in deeply, prickles of cold searing the inside of his lungs. Had he ever been up this early at home? *When living*, he thought ruefully, *as a duke?*

It was as though these early hours had not existed. At least, he had seen them a few times...from the other direction. All too easy when frequenting the Dulverton Club.

But experience them like this? Fresh air, fresh lungs, sharp mind?

That was why his heart was singing, Henry thought as he strode over the village green toward the blacksmith's. The only reason, not a pretty young woman with more strength than he knew what to do with.

"There you are," said Minny without looking up as he stepped into the forge. "I thought I was going to have to send out a search party."

Henry grinned. "Missed me?"

She turned at that remark, a look of sharp reproval in her eyes. "No."

Henry's grin broadened.

Minny Banfield may be the expert on furnaces and chopping wood and smithing and knowing precisely how hard to hit something...

But he knew ladies. He knew all the little patter they liked to hear, the way he could suggest more with his silent eyes than some pups could splutter in twenty minutes.

And he knew what women looked like when they liked what they looked at.

Minny liked him. Of that, he was sure. *The trouble was*, Henry thought wryly, *he liked what he saw, too—far too much.*

That stolen kiss had taken them both by surprise. If he was going to keep his head clear and discover the secrets of this gossiping network, he needed to stay alert.

Stay away from the tempting lips of Minny Banfield.

"So, what is the lesson today?" Henry said, just a touch more formally. He saw her shoulders relax and wished to goodness he could kiss her senseless. "More fire laying?"

It had been an important lesson she had told him repeatedly as Henry had complained of the repetition the last two days.

"Laying a fire in a grate is one thing but laying a fire in a furnace is quite another," she had said only yesterday. "One heats you—but my forge heats me, feeds me, keeps a roof above my head."

"Clever fire," Henry had quipped.

He had earned a gentle nudge on the arm for that. It had been all Henry could manage not to try another quip just to feel her soft fingers against his skin again.

"No, I think we have done fires quite to death," Minny said sweetly. "You took to it quite quickly, in truth."

There was a dancing glint in her eyes that made Henry's mouth fall open. "You—you made me build those fires over and over again, until I—"

"Well, it's not a job I particularly like, I will admit," the laughing woman said as she banked the fire and closed up the furnace. "It was far more pleasant letting you worry about getting all dirty."

Henry shook his with frank amusement. It was difficult not to be impressed. He'd had an inkling, the first few days of his time here, that Minny was merely using him as an errand boy, a boot room boy, like he had at Dulverton Manor.

And here she was, confirming it!

Wiley woman. If only she did not do such a thing with such evident enjoyment of his discomfort and a teasing promise of a kiss on her lips.

Henry's stomach jolted. *Blast. He mustn't think of—*

"Come on," said Minny abruptly, striding out of the forge.

Henry blinked. Then he followed. "Wait—Minny, wait!"

He ran into her as he stepped into the comparatively blinding light of the outdoors.

Thrusting his hands out to prevent himself from toppling over her—not that it would be the end of the world—Henry was rather delighted to find Minny accidentally in his arms.

Her cheeks flushed, her eyes widened. "Henry—"

"Yes?" Henry breathed.

If she thought he was going to release her after she breathed his name, she was very much mistaken. His blood was pounding, temptation rising to the surface, and it was all he could do not to—

"Miss Banfield, good morning!"

Minny stepped away as though she had been scalded. "Reverend Pinkerton! How pleasant to see you."

Henry blinked, trying to get back his bearings. As Minny stepped away, all center of balance had been shaken, his balance knocked. The world seemed off-center, and it took him almost a full minute—while Minny chattered away nonchalantly to the vicar—to find his footing.

"—servant you have there," the Reverend Pinkerton was saying.

Henry's gaze snapped to Minny, who was evidently trying not to laugh. "Oh, he's no servant, sir, he's not nearly clever enough for that. I'm using him as an odd-job man."

A prickle of irritation mingled with delight seared his heart. *Oh, she was, was she?*

He had never been on a teasing footing with a lady before. One learned not to; it could give rise to speculation, and before you knew it, you were tied to her forever after a hasty marriage her father had insisted on.

God forbid he end up falling into that trap.

But this...this was different. As their eyes met, a frisson rocked through him. It was all he could do not to pull Minny away from the polite vicar and demand to know...

Everything. Oh God, he wanted to know everything about her.

Taste every—

"—must be going now," Minny said, interrupting his thoughts. "Come on, Mr. Everleigh."

And she did something he could never have predicted. She slipped her hand into his arm and started walking along the street.

Henry managed to put one foot in front of the other but it was a close run thing. Every iota of his concentration was fixed on the small part of his arm where he and she interconnected. His arm was warm, growing warmer with every step...

Minny walked alongside him as though this was all perfectly natural. There was such elegance, such carefree grace in the way she guided him down a lane, his breath was stolen.

Oh, with a woman like this by his side...

"I must apologize for the Reverend Pinkerton," Minny said airily. "Thinking you were a servant when you are really a miscreant hiding out in my forge, the idea!"

She grinned, and Henry smiled weakly back. *So, that was what she thought, was it?*

"How did you guess?" he said warily.

Minny shrugged as they slowed by what had to be stables, by the smell. "Oh, it was not so difficult. A man with money but no trade, interested in hiding in a blacksmith's in a village in the middle of nowhere? Do you think I'm a fool?"

Henry swallowed. *No, but he was.* That would have been the perfect excuse, of course. It seemed obvious when she said it.

"You won't tell anyone?"

Minny's dancing eyes grew serious for a moment. "It's...well, your life is your own, I say. Whatever mistakes you've made, I'm sure you've paid for them."

Now that was an interesting thought. Mistakes? Henry was not sure he had ever made a mistake in his life. Not a proper one.

Deciding to challenge old Martock to a drinking contest just before he went to France was not a mistake, not really. More the precursor to a fantastic story.

Still, Minny did not know that. For all she knew, he was a danger-ous criminal on the run.

And his heart flickered painfully as she said softly, "I'm not one to punish a man for his nature."

"What do you—"

"Ah, Mr. Anthony, I am sorry for being late, but here we are," said Minny breezily.

She stepped forward to greet the farmer who had appeared in the lane to welcome them. Only then did Henry realize she had slipped her hand from his arm.

The distance between them could only have been a few feet, but it felt an eternity, a painful absence that made no sense.

Henry blinked with astonishment, his mind hardly knowing what to do with itself.

"I said, Mr. Everleigh?"

Henry shook his head as though ridding his ears of water, and saw both ruddy farmer and pretty woman staring. "I beg your pardon?"

Mr. Anthony sniffed. "I see what you mean, Miss."

Oh blast, what had he missed?

"Yes, he's slow on the uptake," said Minny conversationally, grin-ning as she spoke. "But I have found him moderately useful. Now, that stallion of yours. I'd like to see him..."

Henry almost laughed as the three of them entered the stables to inspect one of the farmer's horses. *Slow on the uptake?*

One day he would make Minny pay for...*no*, he thought awkward-ly as he waited outside the stall, allowing Minny to inspect the large cart horse before them.

The Duke of Dulverton could certainly tempt a woman to lose her innocence in his bed...but Henry Everleigh was just a man. A man with a little coin, hiding in a blacksmith's...

Which did not explain why his heart raced so quickly just watching

Minny caress the horse's flank. Why he ached to be the one she was touching. Why he wished the damned farmer would leave them and he could take Minny's hand and lead her to an empty stall and—

"Henry? Henry?"

Henry stared. The farmer had gone—when, he did not know—and Minny was grinning with an all-too-knowing look. "I beg your pardon? My apologies, my mind was otherwise engaged."

She snorted as she patted the stallion. "Where on earth did you learn to speak like that? You sound like someone off the stage!"

He grinned weakly. *Ah, yes.* He really would have to make more of an effort. The last thing he needed, just as Minny decided he was a hopeless case who needed to be protected, was to reveal he was actually a duke and likely as not owned half the village.

That would be rather awkward.

"What are you doing?" he said aloud, ignoring her question.

Minny sighed as she pointed to the hind leg of the horse. "See there, the right one? How he's not putting any weight on it?"

Henry looked. It looked like a horse to him. He may own several dozen horses, but they were things he rode, not animals he had to care for. He'd had a man for that. Three men, now he came to think.

"Someone else shod that horse," Minny said darkly. "Someone who didn't know what they were doing and who has made a complete hash of it. See, the way the shoe has slipped partly from the sole?"

Henry looked. It still looked like a horse to him, but—no, there it was. A slight shine of iron, which surely he should not be able to see. The horse stood there patiently.

"So it…it hurts the horse?" he hazarded.

Minny's knowing smile was difficult to bear. "You've never worked with animals before, have you?"

"Not many people either," Henry confessed.

After all, technically, he was a gentleman. Gentleman did not work.

They…ordered people about. That was about as close as he got.

"Mr. Anthony has apologized of course, but it'll be a few days before the old boy will be able to work again, even after I've reshod him," Minny said with a sigh. "And that will mean havoc for Mr. Smith."

Henry blinked. The village was not large, but he had spent most of his time in the forge. Few people came directly to the blacksmith's, almost as though...well. Now he came to think about it, almost as if they had no wish to go, but were forced to because they needed to.

What was it Ted had said?

"We don't speak of 'im."

"Who is Mr. Smith?"

Minny brushed a straw from the skirt of her gown. Henry tried not to look at the gentle swell of her buttocks underneath the fabric. "Mr. Smith is the miller. With the river so low, he requires a horse to help run the mill, and so without this handsome boy—"

"He can't mill," Henry said slowly.

She nodded. "And that means higher prices for Mr. Lane, of course."

Henry was starting to get a headache with all these names. It did not help that the scent of straw and horses was insufficient to block out the tempting Minny Banfield. "What?"

Minny shook her head ruefully. "You've never lived in a village before, have you?"

Henry's father had once described Dulverton Manor as a village. It was about as large, had just as many inhabitants, and was so full of gossip in the air of the Servants Hall. "No."

She stepped around him, brushing up against him in the most tantalizing way a woman had ever not attempted to get his attention. "Well, Mr. Lane is the baker here at Pathstow. Without local flour, he'll have to buy it—pushing up prices. It means pies at the King's Head will go up a ha'penny, too, which means..."

Henry followed her, dazed, out of the stall and out of the stables.

"You mean to tell me this horse not having the correct horseshoe will affect all that?"

Minny grinned as she slipped her hand into his arm as they started to walk slowly back through the village toward the forge. "Village life, Henry. All the different parts of the place, they all interlock together. One change affects us all."

"I had no idea."

She grinned at his admission. "People need people, Henry."

Henry's stomach swooped. She had slipped into using his first name, how he did not know, but by God, he liked it.

"I've never needed anyone," he said quietly.

For some reason, Minny's hand tightened on his arm. "Really?"

"I mean...well," Henry said awkwardly. "No. Not really. I am my own man, I make my own decisions. Any difficulties I face are therefore my responsibility."

Was it his imagination, or was there a stifled giggle from the woman beside him? "And how is that working out for you, Mr. Henry Everleigh, hiding in my forge?"

A prickle of discomfort rose up his chest. "I...well."

"Besides, I don't believe you," Minny said boldly, confidence rising in her voice. "The coat you wear, the shirt you don, everything you eat, every time you read a newspaper—" Henry's heart skipped a beat "—or listen to a tune...that's come from someone, hasn't it? Someone else wove the fabric, cut it, tailored it. Cooked your food, brewed your ale, printed a story, wrote a song...how can you say you've never needed anyone?"

Henry stared. *How was this poetry spilling from the lips of a woman blacksmith?*

Minny seemed to guess his thoughts—at least, in part. She flushed. "I just mean, everyone needs everyone, that's how the world works. It would be a lonely life, I think, to be entirely separate. Don't you think?"

And only then did Henry realize just how lonely he had been. Yes, Minny was right; his life had been created and dictated by servants all around him, but when did he ever bare his soul? How often was he vulnerable, truly open with his friends? When had he last—

"Henry?"

He smiled down at the concerned woman. "Yes?"

"You...you looked..." Minny hesitated.

They had come to a stop just outside the forge, and Henry was highly conscious they were still arm in arm. Almost as though...they were courting.

"I thought I saw, in your eyes...it was nothing," she said hastily. "Come on. I've got a fire needs lighting, and I know just the man."

Henry groaned as she slipped from his grasp. "You mean I still can't hit anything?"

CHAPTER EIGHT

April 15, 1810

M INNY HEAVED A sigh as she placed the final nail on the bench. "And that's the last."

She almost laughed at the look of relief on his face.

"Are you sure?"

"Quite sure," Minny said, opening the furnace and the kitchen door to allow the heat to pour through. It was one of the few benefits of living so close to the forge. She never had to worry about the cold in the winter.

Henry collapsed onto the stool, almost missing it in his haste. "Oh, dear Lord, I thought we'd never get there!"

"It wasn't that large an order, really," Minny said, carefully placing back her tools as she wiped her forehead with the back of her hand. "Just one hundred nails…"

A groan muffled her words. "And you call that a small order!"

Minny looked at the man who had somehow become just as much a part of the forge as her leather apron or the heavy gloves or her order book.

Henry Everleigh. To think, she had been so determined to keep him out of the forge…

"I am sorry, Mr. Everleigh, but there is no apprentice position available at

STRIKE WHILE THE DUKE IS HOT

my forge. Goodbye."

Now she rather wondered how she had managed to keep the place going without him. All that wood chopping may have brought down his pride a little, but it also had kept her furnace well heated for weeks now.

She hadn't been able to lift the plough that Farmer Jones had sent. Without Henry, she would not have been able to placate Mr. Anthony's stallion when it came in yesterday—how he had known how to calm a horse, she did not know. He had not explained.

The trouble was, Minny told herself darkly as she cleaned the last of the hammers and placed it back in its position on the wall, *she was getting too accustomed to him.*

Her heart contracted painfully as she looked back at the handsome man, his hair darker thanks to the grime of their day's work.

How long would she have him?

How long, she corrected, *would he be here?* For he was not hers; he owed her nothing, and she certainly owed him even less.

But the idea he could leave, suddenly disappear...

Minny had always told herself she would never be dependent on someone again, not after...

But that had been before Henry Everleigh had arrived at her door.

"You'll be heading back to the King's Head, I suppose," she found herself saying.

Henry shrugged, the muscles in his strong arms flexing as he did so. "I suppose so—unless you have a meal for me here?"

Minny's breath caught in her throat. It was a line they had never crossed. They worked hard, him perhaps harder than her, now she knew she could relieve some of the burden from her shoulders. They laughed together. She was altogether far too conscious of Henry's body...

And then he said that. Easily, as though he suggested they eat together all the time.

Well, they did have lunch together, Minny tried to tell herself, as her throat closed up and all thoughts of how to respond vanished. At least, what he called "luncheon."

She had fair laughed when he first said that. Bread, meat, and whatever vegetables she could find that hadn't gone moldy in the store was hardly "luncheon"!

But there was no reason, Minny thought wistfully, *he could not stay for dinner.* It was not as though there was anything particularly scandalous in it. They would be alone, to be sure, but then…they were always alone.

"Minny…"

Minny swallowed. *She was not,* she thought firmly, *going to think about that kiss.* The kiss. The kiss that had awakened something in her she did not understand—could not understand without speaking of it to someone.

And who else was there?

"Minny?"

"What?" she said distractedly, Henry coming into focus. "Yes, a food—I mean, of course. You can stay. If you want."

There was something odd crystalizing in the air between them.

A smile threatened to dismantle all her self-control. That was, she would very much like to put her finger on what it was, but touching Henry Everleigh was surely a recipe for disaster…

"Excellent," said Henry, slapping his hands together and rubbing them. "What shall it be? Lord save me from a pork pie, I believe that is the only sustenance the King's Head offers."

Minny giggled as she removed her leather apron, carefully folded it, and started toward the kitchen. "Sustenance?"

"Food—you know what I mean," said Henry good naturedly as he followed her.

He was a strange one, with his peculiar words and funny phrases. But Minny could not think on that. Not with Henry stepping into the kitchen, his looming presence making the place feel small.

It had felt perfectly serviceable when she was a child. It was just her father and Alan and herself for so long, and her brother had left—escaped, he'd called it—when she had been...what. Twelve?

So it had only been the two of them. The older man had never taken up much room.

Minny swallowed. Not like Henry Everleigh.

She did not know how he did it, but the man always seemed to take up so much more...space than any other man. He was tall yes, and broader than herself, but that did not go all the way to explaining just how present he was in a room.

As though he was sucking in all the air, preventing anyone from breathing. Or was that just her?

"What can I do?" Henry said eagerly, leaning against the small table and sliding it a few inches. "Whoops!"

Minny tried not to stare. *How strong was this man, if the mere act of leaning could shift the old oak table?*

"You," she said sternly, "can sit."

Like a dog newly trained, Henry sat obediently. Right down on the floor.

Minny tried to stifle her giggles. "Were you always this troublesome?"

"No, it's something new you've bred into me," said Henry cheerfully, stretching out his legs. He was so tall; he almost stretched the full length of the little room. "Are you sure I cannot—"

"Wood," Minny said with a wry smile. That was one of the surprising things about Henry; he liked to be doing things. The moment he realized he could do something, he was itching to do it.

Not a common feature in the men of Pathstow.

"Now, you can tell me all about the village gossip you've heard in the King's Head," said Minny with a mischievous grin after he brought in a few more logs. "While I chop."

It was remarkably pleasant. As the sun slipped below the horizon and the two candles on each side of the kitchen were lit, Minny chopped vegetables while listening to Henry chatter away.

His ease at storytelling was something she had never encountered before. Though he had been here less than a month, he appeared to be on speaking terms with half the village and on gossiping terms with the rest.

"—and there'll be a scandal, I suppose, if they do not wed," Henry said with a raised eyebrow. "You know how gossip can spread."

Minny's jaw tightened. "I do indeed."

The forge extended into the kitchen with another small door so she could place the large cooking pot within. Her fingers only slightly stumbled as she tried not to think about the gossip which had forced her brother to leave Pathstow.

Oh, if only he had...well, it was all water under the bridge now. He could never come back. Not truly.

He had done too much to be forgiven, it seemed. Which was why the letters—

"And how long will that take?" Henry said eagerly.

Minny didn't answer. "Minny?"

"What?" she said distractedly.

Henry was grinning. "What were you thinking of just now?"

Her cheeks flamed. "Nothing."

"You were thinking of something," he teased, rising to his feet and stepping toward her. "Do you not think we are good enough friends for you to tell me?"

Minny looked into the handsome face of the man she trusted implicitly, despite all evidence telling her not to.

She was alone here. He could do anything to her—not that she thought he would hurt her, but still...she was alone. And he was running from something; she had worked that much out herself.

If he had not have kissed her, she would have wondered...

"Minny?"

"Nothing," she repeated, stepping away from the little door to the forge.

Yes, that was why she was burning up. That had to be the reason. Not because she had just imagined reaching out and touching...

Minny was grateful that Henry stepped back and sat at the table, hands folded. He started to talk about another exciting piece of gossip from the village—a pair of twins, newly born—and she could relax.

By the time the stew was ready, Minny had almost collected herself. *He was just a man,* she told herself. A man she was alone with. That was why she felt...odd in his presence.

Pride seared her heart as she served up a healthy portion of stew in one of the few unchipped bowls. She may not be the sort of woman a man would take to wife—she had long ago accepted she would never marry, not as a blacksmith—but that did not mean she couldn't feed a man.

She watched, eagle eyed, as Henry dipped his spoon into the dish and brought it to his mouth.

And grinned as his eyes widened.

"Good God, this is—"

"Not too hot?" Minny asked sweetly, dishing up her own bowl.

Henry shook his head. "You know it is delicious, don't you?"

"Well, I have had a little practice," Minny said, seating herself opposite. "One doesn't make stew over and over again for ten years or so without—"

"Ten years?"

For some reason, Henry looked more astonished than when he had tasted her delicious stew—which was odd.

Minny was not *that* old. Almost one and twenty, a perfectly respectable age. What daughter did not start helping her mother as she reached her tenth birthday, if not before?

"Yes, ten years," she said, a mite defensively. "Why?"

Henry was staring as though he had never seen her before. "But...I mean to say, you cannot be more than twenty!"

"One and twenty," said Minny with a frown as she had another mouthful of her stew. *Oh goodness, it was good.* "And?"

"But...but..." spluttered Henry, frowning as if a complex calculation had been presented to him. "But that would mean you were working in the kitchen from the age of—"

"Ten, yes, just like every daughter in this whole village, I'll be bound," Minny said with a dry laugh.

Why was he looking at her like that?

"Look, I don't see what's so unusual about it," she said, her hackles rising. "I mean, what sort of daughter would I be if I wasn't helping my mother? Everyone does it, surely where you grew up—"

"My sister would never," Henry began stiffly before his eyes widened. "I mean...if Peg..."

Minny leaned closer, curiosity overcoming her surprise at his pomposity. There was that sister again. Was that who he would return to when he was finished here? Or was there a wife?

Her cheeks darkened. *Well.* He had not mentioned one, and she would hope a married man would not be kissing her like that. So why had his sister not—

"...I just think ten years old is young, that's all," Henry said weakly. "Should you not have...I do not know, been in school?"

Minny examined him closely. *Where had this man come from? A village where children did not help their parents? Most strange.*

"School?" she repeated. "What school?"

Henry stared. "But there must be a school!"

"Why? Most villages around here have no school—oh, there's the poorhouse school for boys at the town over the way, and Sunday school of course, but an actual school?" Minny scoffed. "We'd need a great more guineas to afford that!"

"But—ten years old! That's so young!"

"I don't think so," she said bluntly, knowing it was most unseemly to be so direct but unable to help herself. "I mean, some of us applied to work up at the manor at that age, and though Jane was the only one who secured a place, we all wanted the work. I mean, it's not like lords and ladies don't put us to work," she said with a laugh. "Why not our own mothers!"

Minny had expected him to laugh, to nod and admit she was right. But instead, he blanched, his face turning white. Henry looked at his stew and swallowed.

What had got into him?

"But—"

"Henry, when did you start working?"

Minny had not intended the question to feel a cross examination, but curiosity overwhelmed her good manners.

What was this man? Someone who believed that children should not work, should not help in the home—that every child, even those of a poor villager, should attend school?

"I..." Henry swallowed. He took several mouthfuls of stew, then said, "I suppose my father included me in the...the family business when I turned fourteen or so."

Minny raised an eyebrow. "That was late. Youngest child?"

"Eldest of two."

"And the family business is?"

Perhaps it was Minny's imagination, but the closer she looked at Henry, the more discomforted he looked. Was it possible...she had only been teasing really when she had suggested that he had fled a criminal past, but could it be true?

Tendrils of distress curled around her chest, tightening her lungs. *Had she invited a criminal into her forge, her kitchen...her life?*

"Land management, I suppose you would say," Henry said eventually, pushing back the bowl, now empty. "That was the best thing I have ever tasted."

Minny grinned, her heart warming at the flattery. "It's just stew."

Did he think she would be so easily distracted by a compliment that she would not ask—

"I suppose hard work makes it taste better," Henry said with a shrug. "Or perhaps it is the company."

As the twinkle in his eyes continued and his hands remained on the table, deliciously close to her own, heat flushed her cheeks.

He was...flirting! With her!

She dropped her gaze to her half-eaten stew. "Perhaps this wasn't a good idea."

"The stew? I think it was a delightful idea."

Oh, he was jesting, surely! How could he not see the...the potential dangers here!

As Minny looked up, she saw a crease on Henry's forehead, the way his body tensed against the chair. Oh, he knew. He just had no wish to admit it, quite a different thing altogether.

The kitchen appeared to be smaller again. All it contained was him, and her, and the table between them.

Thank goodness she had not thought to sit beside him...

"You know what I mean," Minny said quietly. "I don't think this was a good idea."

She forced herself to look up, but all that achieved was a delightful swooping of her stomach as her eyes met his. They were fierce, determined in a way she was already starting to associate with the tall man.

There was a fire within him, hotter than a forge. The question was, what did he want?

Henry hesitated, then said, "I...I know what you mean. I think."

"I mean, I am unmarried and alone here with you," Minny said, the words rushing from her mouth as her cheeks darkened with heat. "There could be talk, I could lose my reputation!"

"We have done nothing but work—"

"You kissed me," said Minny quietly.

Oh, if only her entire body did not have to crimson at the words. What had provoked her to say them?

Only the desperate desire to have it confirmed that she had not dreamt the encounter. Only the need to know whether he had also thought about it. Dreamt about it—

"Why aren't you married?" Minny asked quietly.

It was an absolutely scandalous question to ask, but that no longer seemed to matter. He was here, wasn't he? Any chatter in the village would undoubtedly increase now he had spent the evening here.

Had dinner here, Minny corrected silently.

The question echoed around the kitchen. Henry did not immediately fill the awkward silence.

When he did speak, it was in a slow, measured tone that told Minny just how carefully he had considered his words.

"I suppose I always worried about my sister's marriage more than mine. The idea of marrying before Pegs...she's my responsibility, you see. I can think on my own marriage, my own pleasure, once she is secure."

Though she flushed at the word "pleasure," Minny leaned forward curiously. "It is only the two of you, then?"

Henry nodded. "I'm all she has, worse luck for her."

"Oh, I think you are far better for her than many brothers could have been," said Minny with feeling before she could stop herself. At Henry's curious glance, she added, "I mean...I would not mind you for a brother."

She cringed inwardly at the foolishness of her words. *What had possessed her to say such a thing!*

Her hands were still on the table, as were Henry's. In a movement slow and steady, as though inviting her to withdraw her hand at any time, he moved his hand closer to hers.

Minny's breath caught in her throat. She needed to move away, away from the table—she needed to tell him to return to the King's Head! But she could not.

Henry's warm fingers captured her own, and Minny gasped. Oh, the intimacy of that small action, the sense of his fingers around hers.

Here they sat, alone in the candlelit gloom. Her pulse was racing, heart thundering, and desire, desire Minny knew she should ignore rushed through her veins.

"The trouble is," Henry said in a low voice, eyes fixed on hers. "The last way...the very last way I would wish you to consider me is that of a brother."

Minny's voice caught in her throat. She could do nothing, say nothing, move not an inch. The table was not wide, if she leaned forward and he did also, their lips would touch. He could kiss her again, and she could show him just—

"Let me help you clear up," said Henry, releasing her hand and rising from the table.

Minny blinked. The intensity was gone, but she was still moving in a cloud of intoxication. *Clear up?* The last thing she wanted to do was wash up bowls.

No, what she wanted to do was far too scandalous to voice.

Praying her legs would hold her and that her voice would remain steady, she nodded with a wry smile. "Yes. Yes, good. Clear up. That's what we should do."

CHAPTER NINE

April 19, 1810

HENRY GLARED AT the paper in his hands, as though if he did so sufficiently, the damned thing would burst into flames. Not just this edition, either. No, all of them—he had to stop anyone from reading this utter filth!

DUKE'S SISTER SLIPS AWAY FROM BALL TO ATTEND GAMING HELL

It is our sorry duty to report that Lady Margaret Everleigh, sister to the Duke of Dulverton—who appears to have no interest in calming his sister's ways and is absent from Town—was spotted leaving the ill-reputed gaming hell the Old Duke last night.

Despite being chaperoned to Almack's by the devastatingly beautiful Lady Romeril, Lady Margaret appeared to have slipped her clutches.

After dancing twice with the Earl of Thornfalcone, a suggestion of a potential union between the two great houses, voucher holders were astonished to discover Lady Margaret was, sadly, undiscoverable for the latter portion of the evening.

We can now exclusively reveal the reason for this outrage: because she had escaped to the Old Duke, a gaming hell frequented by the most odious characters. Two fights are known to have broken out that evening, though the Duke of Ashcott decently refused to confirm whether one was over the Lady Margaret's honor.

It would seem to this editor that neither could be, because the Lady Margaret has no honor left.

Henry screwed up the newspaper and threw it into the flames. He watched, face livid, as the ends of the paper curled, fire licking the edges.

The bloody fools! What did they think they would achieve, publishing such scandalous lies! Why did they think they could get away with it?

His hands became fists as he sat on the end of his bed in the small room at the King's Head.

The trouble was, they *were* getting away with it, weren't they? Every day that passed when he did not stride up to their damned headquarters and put a bullet through their chest, this editor just kept on publishing.

It was an outrage!

And every day that he stayed here, it was only going to get worse. Why, he had been impressed Lady Romeril had acted as Peggy's companion—there was no one who could get around Lady Romeril. She was a stalwart of Society, no one would dare to besmirch her name.

Except that they had. Henry could not understand it.

At least now Lady Romeril had been dragged into this mess, he hoped she would try to rein in the nonsense coming from this rag of a newspaper. Perhaps she would succeed where Henry had failed.

He smiled weakly, shaking his head. Not that he had been trying very hard.

Somehow, and he was still not sure how, he had managed to slip into the most awkward habit of...becoming a blacksmith.

If his father could see him now!

"I still think I should have a go with the hammer," he had said to Minny yesterday.

And she had laughed. "The moment you can hit an anvil without hitting your own thumb, let me know."

Henry looked ruefully at the cotton wrapped and tied around his left thumb. *Well, it wasn't completely his fault, was it?*

If only he had not been intending to show off quite so dramatically. Then he would not have dropped the hammer so quickly, or forgotten to move his thumb…

"Part of me wonders whether you half did it on purpose," Minny had said as she had bandaged him up.

And Henry had swallowed, trying not to focus on the warm, deft hands that carefully tied the knot in the cotton. And he had wondered, too.

Was it possible that his mind had permitted him to become injured, to give him the perfect excuse to be close to her? To breathe Minny in, wonder what would happen if he once again pulled her into his arms and—

"Henry?"

Henry started, his swift rising almost made him tumble onto the bed.

Minny was standing in the doorway, a smile broadening as she watched him stagger. "Goodness, what's wrong with you? Faint from all that loss of blood?"

He grinned weakly. "Something like that."

He certainly felt weak. How long could he continue being this close to Minny without doing something about it?

Doing something about it? Henry swallowed, knowing he was being foolish. He was the Duke of Dulverton! He was on the pursuit of the blaggards ruining his sister's life!

The absolute last thing he should be thinking of was a pretty face…

"Wh-What?"

Minny giggled. Though Henry desperately hoped she would step inside, she lingered by the doorway—evidently feeling, as he should, that to do so would be most unseemly.

This was his bedchamber. At least, one of the bedchambers at the King's Head. But still. Henry knew enough about etiquette to know it would be deeply outrageous if she—

Minny stepped inside and closed the door behind her. "You're late."

It was all he could do to prevent his jaw from dropping to the ground. *Late?* He had almost expired when she shut that door.

What did she think she was doing? Had their conversation, albeit brief, about her reputation not made any impact? *Was she*, and here Henry's stomach lurched, *was she offering herself to him?*

Because if so, he could not accept swiftly enough—

"I expected you in the forge an hour ago," Minny said quietly.

Ah. That was the trouble with leaving one's pocket watch with one's manservant, Henry thought wretchedly. He hoped Jenks had kept it wound, for he would be in sore need of it when he returned home.

Whenever that was.

"Henry?"

"Yes, I—I am sorry, Minny. Miss Banfield," Henry said awkwardly.

He had no wish to use her formal name, but he did not have much choice.

They were standing here, in a bedchamber—*his bedchamber!*—without a chaperone.

Not, he thought darkly, eyes flickering back to the newspaper now almost ashes in the grate, *that a chaperone seemed to make much difference to protecting a woman's reputation.*

"Miss Banfield?" Minny's face was astonished. "Goodness, I thought we were—it was my mistake, I shouldn't have—"

"No, Minny, I—blast, I don't know," Henry said, stepping forward.

He shouldn't have. Every inch he grew closer, it was impossible to keep control. Her enthralling presence was playing havoc with his restraint, his fingers itching to—

"You don't know?" she repeated, eyes wide.

Henry forced himself to halt, tightened his fingers into fists, and took a deep breath. He needed to remain calm.

Though he had spent almost every day since arriving at Pathstow in her presence, he had still not noticed any opportunity she may have had to sneak letters out to London. She'd made deliveries, naturally, but as far as Henry could see, there were no hidden notes wrapped around the horse shoes, or under belt buckles, or within the packet of nails.

But Peg was depending on him, and as much as it made his gut clench to consider it...Minny Banfield may be his enemy.

Henry had to remember a pretty face did not guarantee innocence.

"Henry? Mr. Everleigh?"

Henry blinked. Minny had stepped closer and was waving a hand before his eyes. He had evidently become lost in his thoughts.

"Don't ever," he said quietly, warmth suffusing into his voice, "call me Mr. Everleigh again."

She looked surprised but pleased. "Really?"

Henry nodded. *Oh, the things he wanted her to call him...* "Henry is fine. What was I saying?"

"You know, I haven't the faintest idea," said Minny, a small smile creasing her lips.

And that was when Henry's heart skipped a beat.

Oh, damn.

He hadn't felt this way since...*well, never,* Henry thought wildly as he tried and failed to collect himself. Even Miss Ahlberg, the governess who had made him tongue tied whenever he tried to explain a mathematical equation, had not made him feel like this.

So warm he felt steam rising from his forehead, his face surely blotchy. Yet so cold, so alone, so separated from the one person who could make him feel whole again.

Dear God, if the memory of one kiss and his name on her lips could make him feel like this, what was he going to do?

"Well, I was worried, after you did not arrive this morning," Minny said a shake of her head. "I suppose I should be giving you a day off every Sunday, but—"

"No," Henry said hurriedly. Spending an entire day away from Minny felt like a punishment somehow.

"Well, that's good. Good."

Henry's traitorous heart skipped a beat again.

He was not here, in the pokey little village of Pathstow, to have his head turned by a blacksmith! Even if this one was comely beyond compare and laughed like the devil when he had knocked over a pair of toasting forks a few days ago.

He had never given his heart to anyone before, and he was not about to do so now. Even if he wished to.

He should leave. Henry was no fool; he'd seen this slippery slope before, seen the way affection could play havoc with a gentleman's focus.

Why, hadn't old Braedon gone absolutely round the twist when he started to fixate on that Miss Tilbury?

There were more important things at stake, Henry tried to tell himself, *than the potential bedding of a delicious woman.* There was his sister to think of, her reputation.

So why was he considering attracting the attentions of a woman blacksmith—one who could quite easily be the culprit of his sister's disgrace?

By God, but she was beautiful.

"Henry?"

"What?" he said. "What did you say?"

"I said," said Minny patiently, "are you ready to learn your first blacksmithing?"

Henry's eyes widened. She laughed as he spluttered, "T-Truly—you think I'm ready?"

And just like that, all his fine feelings were gone. A chance to be with Minny, to see her at work again, see her talent in action—perhaps get close to her...

And best of all, the chance to hit something incredibly hard with a large hammer?

Henry was a man, not an angel. He could not help himself. "That would be wonderful!"

"As ready as you will ever be, and I think I am as ready as I will ever be for you to play near the flames," Minny said dryly. "Honestly, with a thumb in a bandage like that, we'll have to be careful you don't set yourself alight!"

"Let's go," he said impetuously. "Come on, we're wasting time!"

"You were the one who was late!" she protested as she followed him out of his bedchamber.

Henry's heart hammered painfully as he raced down the stairs, almost tripping over the last one before he raced out of the King's Head.

"What the—"

Ted's words fell behind him as Henry grabbed Minny's hand. "Come on!"

"Henry—wait!"

Filled with a rush of energy, of excitement, throwing all caution to the wind and caring not who saw them as they raced across the village green, Henry pulled Minny along.

Their laughter echoed around the small forge when they finally arrived, Henry clutching at his chest, a stitch burning as he looked into the flushed face of Minny Banfield.

"One of these days you'll get me into trouble, Henry," she gasped.

Henry bit back the retort that he greatly wished to. It wouldn't be fair on her, after all, for she had no idea she was running about with a duke.

"Now, the fire will have died down in the time that I went to fetch you," said Minny, turning immediately to business and opening the furnace. "Yes, we'll need a few more logs and any coal still in the scuttle…"

It took the pair of them a while to heat the furnace again, Henry wiping sweat from his brow. Only when Minny nodded and declared it warm enough did he permit himself a rush of excitement.

"So, I can try?"

It was foolish of him to become so eager, Henry knew—but there was something primal about the anvil, about its transformative power, about the way it could take broken or formless things and transform them into something else.

The fact that Minny was pulling on a leather apron and looking at him with a wise and calculating eye certainly did not hurt.

"You can try," she said quietly with a knowing smile. "But remember, this craft is hot."

Henry swallowed as she brushed hair from her eyes. He certainly felt unusually warm as he stood on the other side of the anvil, but he wasn't sure that was what she actually meant.

"Hot," he repeated unnecessarily.

As though she could read his thoughts, Minny flushed. "I-I mean…just, pay attention."

She picked up a lump of iron and a hammer and started to show him how to heat it first in the fire and then use the hammer to gently mold it.

Henry watched, transfixed. If he had been impressed with Minny before, it was nothing to how he felt now.

How was it possible for her to so easily transmute what appeared to be nothing more than a lump of metal into something that had life, movement, potential? Her fingers curled elegantly around the tool, twisting it in small adjustments almost without thinking. Henry was transfixed.

It was therefore rather a surprise when she looked up and handed him the hammer. "There you go."

"What, now?" Henry said instinctively, taking the hammer but holding it hesitantly, as though it would be taken from him at any moment.

Minny's cheeks were flushed—*from the heat of the furnace*, Henry told himself—as she grinned. "Is this not what you came for? Is this not what you want?"

His mouth went dry. *What he wanted?*

Oh, what he wanted…

If someone had asked him a month ago, he would have known the answer. He wanted to bring the people who harmed his sister to justice.

But now, with Minny smiling, trusting, believing him to be nothing but a man who wished to learn from her…

He had entered her life under false pretenses. Now he wished for nothing more than to push aside the warm metal and lay Minny on the forge floor and show her such pleasure that she would never be able to look at another man again.

"Henry?"

Not that he could admit to such a thing.

"Right. Yes. This is what I want," he said aloud, as though verbalizing it would make it more true. "Fine, so, you just hit it like this—"

The gentle movement of the hammer clanged around the forge, and a rush of excitement poured through Henry's lungs. *Oh, this was spectacular! The sense of power!*

He hit it again, felt the rush of vibration through his arm, tilted his wrist to hit it again.

"Oh, this is easy!"

"That's what they tell me," Minny said dryly.

And it was that moment when Henry lost all concentration. He looked at Minny—and his hand slipped.

Not the one holding the hammer. That would certainly have been painful, but that hand stayed steady.

No, it was his other hand, leaning on the anvil, that jerked to the right as he looked at her. Unable to help himself, Henry's heart lurched in a way he had never felt before and his hand responded in turn...

"Oh, ye gods!"

...straight into the fizzing iron on the center of the anvil.

Henry immediately brought his fingers to his mouth. Certain as he was that Minny would have performed the deed if required, as she had with his wrist weeks earlier, the last thing his meager self-control needed in this moment was her lips around his fingers.

He closed his eyes with a moan. *Dear God, even thinking about it...*

"You are hurt—is it very bad?" came the anxious voice of the blacksmith who had, arguably, been fool enough to permit him to have a go.

Henry slowly opened his eyes, hoping his self-discipline would return.

His heart skipped a beat. He was in trouble, far more trouble than he had thought when she had turned up at his bedchamber at the King's Head. Far more trouble than he had ever been.

Oh, his head had been turned before by a pretty face, but that had been all. A turn. He had soon returned to his life, his family, his friends, and never thought about the woman.

But this...this was different.

"That is what happens," said Minny, seeing he was in no real danger, "when one does not pay attention."

Henry could do nothing but speak hoarsely. "I was distracted."

"Distracted? Distracted by what?"

There were no words. Henry merely looked at her, trying both to communicate all he felt with his eyes, simultaneously trying to hide the rush of emotions he had not yet untangled.

Minny's cheeks flamed red. "Oh."

Henry swallowed. He was in danger here, real danger. The question was, what would boil over first: his latent desire that was becoming less latent with every passing second, or the blisters on his skin?

CHAPTER TEN

April 23, 1810

M INNY WINCED.

"You said I could—"

"I did not say you could do it wrong," she said with a laugh. Another mistake, just like the one a few days ago. *Did the man never learn?* "Honestly, have you ever seen me do that?"

Henry looked up, sweat beaded on his brow, face flushed by the furnace. "No?"

It was all she could do not to laugh. Honestly, she had known this was too difficult for the man. After first giving him an opportunity to take to the anvil days ago, Minny had known it would be a slow race, Henry's confidence with a hammer.

After all, he had burnt himself almost immediately.

But that had been then, and this was now. Henry had insisted he had learned from his mistake—Minny was still trying to forget the searing way he had looked at her, as though he was taking off her clothes piece by piece—and it was impossible to say no to this man.

Minny swallowed. There she was, letting her thoughts get away from her again. It was getting harder and harder to concentrate with Henry Everleigh in her life and in her forge.

Leaning back on the stool, she tried to watch Henry coolly without noticing the flex of the muscle in his arms, or the way his eyes focused so closely on the iron on the anvil he was attempting to work.

This afternoon they had agreed he would have another try on the anvil, and to his credit, he was doing...not badly. She would never hit at that strange angle, but she was not the one this time getting distracted...

"What are you doing?" Henry asked without looking up.

Minny's gaze hastily dropped to the notebook in her hands. "Nothing—working on the accounts."

It was true. At least, it would have been true if she was actually doing the accounts and not getting distracted by the handsome man.

Who knew, she thought mischievously, a spark of heat rushing through her, *that Henry would look so...so impressive up there, by the anvil?*

There was something so delectable about a man put to work.

She swallowed. What she should be doing is writing to Alan. That had been her intention; it had been a few weeks since she had passed on the last letter. She needed to write a note to go around it and place it by the trough once Henry had returned to the King's Head.

The trouble was, her pencil had ceased its scratching almost the moment Henry had removed his waistcoat.

Dear Alan—I am delighted to say

Minny glanced down at the paltry words she had managed to scribble, then back to the handsome man.

Henry grinned. "Any more critique you wish to throw my way?"

"You must always strike while the metal is hot, always—see, it has cooled too much already."

She could tell from here. It was only a distance of six feet or so, but her eye was carefully attuned to the way metal looked, or more importantly, sounded.

Her father had always said that if he lost his sight, he'd be able to continue just based on the sizzle of the metal, the way the hammer rang throughout the forge.

Henry's forehead crinkled. "How can you possibly know from there?"

A surge of confidence rushed through Minny. "Try hitting it now."

He did so. "The damned thing is cold!"

"Did I, or did I not, just say that?"

Their laughter filled the forge. Minny impetuously wished that it would never cease.

She had never permitted herself to consider herself lonely. She had certainly felt lonely, but tried to tell herself time and time again that it would be too dangerous having someone else about the place.

Alan's secret was safe with her, and she would never betray him. But it would be difficult having someone else in the forge day in and day out who did not know.

But somehow, though of course she was careful, that particular problem had never reared its head with Henry.

She felt...safe with him. And at the same time, more in danger than she ever had been in her life.

Henry had thrust the iron into the furnace, watching, as she had taught him, for the way the metal changed color as it heated. Just as it was perfectly suited to a little light hammering, Minny watched as he moved it from the flames to the anvil.

Clang!

He tapped it gently, then more forcefully. Minny watched surreptitiously, pretending to be writing but instead watching the way he learned, fingers twisting the hammer to gain greater purchase.

When he had first arrived, his hands had been soft. It had been all Minny could do not to dream of them on her skin after that reckless kiss they had shared.

His story about being a land manager with his father was surely true, then. Henry Everleigh had been a man who had worked, perhaps, but not with his hands.

No longer. Minny's gaze drifted to Henry's hands, his rough palms, the burned and scarred wrist, the way his calloused fingers gripped tightly. He had hardened, yes, but he only seemed to melt her more.

What would it be to feel those calloused fingers stroking her—

"Minny?"

"What?" she said hurriedly, closing the notebook on her pencil and looking up eagerly.

Any excuse to look at him was one worth taking.

Henry's smile was too knowing. "You're looking at me."

Minny's lips quirked. "You said my name."

"I meant before that. When you were pretending to be writing, writing…whatever it is that you're writing."

Her cheeks flushed. Minny was not about to admit she had been looking at him, that would be outrageous. Young women did not look at men. *The very idea!*

Except she had been.

"No, I wasn't," she said automatically. *Well, it would hardly be right just to admit it, would it?*

Henry seemed to know what she was thinking. He grinned as he pushed back his hair. "I know what I saw, Minny Banfield, and it was you, looking at me."

Minny swallowed. She greatly enjoyed looking at him, more's the pity. If only the Henry Everleigh who had turned up at her forge had been old, dull, so uninteresting she could have sent him on his way with no regrets.

But he was a part of her life now. That did not mean, however, that she was going to merely accept his aspersions.

Minny drew herself up as best she could on the stool and promised herself she would complete her note to Alan later. "I was inspecting your technique."

Henry's eyebrows raised. "My technique?"

She nodded, unsure why the words made her heart flutter. "Yes, I had to look at your hands t-to see how you were holding the hammer."

It sounded a poor excuse, even to her ears. Minny dropped her gaze, unable to continue looking into the handsome face of a man she knew she could not have.

Would not have. Unless…unless he truly wished to learn the ways of blacksmithing, her traitorous heart could not help but whisper. Unless when his money ran out, he decided to stay. Marry her. Become a part of the forge, just as she was.

Minny swallowed, wishing to goodness her stomach would not insist in tying itself in knots.

She was being ridiculous.

"Besides," she found herself saying, smile returning as she lifted her head. "You would only know I was looking at you if you were looking at me."

And there it was—the sudden flush, the way Henry looked away then immediately back.

He was embarrassed, too! He had been looking, hoping, perhaps, for her attention.

Desire rushed through her, and Minny did nothing this time to push it back.

Was it not clear they liked each other? She hardly had the words for it; she had never been courted, the sudden death of her father putting paid to all thoughts of matrimony. She'd had the forge to look after. Her brother, the fool, to care for.

Was this what it was, to meet someone you wished to court?

Odd courtship, Minny could not help but think, throat dry in the heat of the forge. Why, if they had been lords and ladies, there would already be a scandal. They had been alone together so often. He had even kissed her!

"I was only looking at you because you were looking at me," Henry shot back hastily.

Minny raised an eyebrow, desire compelling the boldness so often reticent within her. "Is that a fact?"

Their gazes held for a heart-stopping moment, one that stole Minny's breath and made it impossible to think.

"You know, it is remarkably hot in here."

Minny blinked. She must have imagined that—it was the sort of tawdry thing a milkmaid would say!

But then, the words had apparently not come from her mouth.

Henry's eyes blazed with fire. Though they reflected the flames of the furnace, there was something else there, something wild and dark and wonderful. Something fixed on Minny that nailed her to the stool, unable to move.

Though what she would have done, she could not tell. Particularly when, without releasing her from his gaze, Henry very slowly placed the hammer on the anvil and pulled her leather apron over his head.

"Wh-What are you—"

"I said, it was remarkably hot in here," said Henry steadily. "Don't you agree?"

Minny's stomach was twisting so wildly, she was certain he could hear it—but then her heart was beating so loudly, perhaps that was drowning it out.

This was a trap, yet Henry's eyes tempted her beyond anything she could endure.

Whatever was about to happen, she wanted it, could feel the aching need between her legs.

"I...yes, quite warm I would say, but—Henry!"

Minny had been unable to help herself. Exclaiming his name, however, did not make him cease the absolutely outrageous thing he was doing.

He was removing his shirt.

Minny blinked several times, sure that each time she opened her eyes, she would see she had been mistaken—but no.

Slowly, without taking his eyes from her save for the brief moment the linen fabric obscured his face, Henry pulled up his shirt to reveal taut and hair speckled muscles.

The shirt fell to the floor.

Henry stood by the anvil, still looking intensely at Minny, certain she was going to melt from this stool onto the floor. How could she not? Knots of desire were untangling in her chest, between her legs, making her mouth dry and her hands wish to know desperately what those muscles felt like.

Dear God, he was so attractive, it was surely criminal!

Heat flushed through Minny's face as she rose, notebook and pencil falling to the floor. She ignored them.

"Right," she said faintly, stepping around the anvil as though this was a perfectly normal day, and she absolutely wasn't approaching a half-naked man in her forge. "Right."

"I hope you don't mind," Henry said, a teasing smile dancing across his lips as he spoke seriously. "It helps to keep cool, as you can imagine. And it is remarkably hot in here."

"Remarkably so," breathed Minny, coming to stop just before him.

He turned to face her, the anvil to the side, giving her clear access to—

Minny forced her hand to return to her side. *This was not happening!* Handsome, muscular men did not pay to be in her forge, play with her anvil, then start removing their clothes!

Except they did. At least, Henry did.

And now she could not draw her eyes away from the hair scattering down his neck, his chest, toward his breeches—

Minny swallowed, hoping to goodness she had not whimpered aloud. She was no expert, far from it, but there appeared to be a...well. A large iron rod within his breeches.

"You're still looking at me," Henry breathed.

Minny's eyes snapped to his face. "I...I am?"

He nodded.

She tried to breathe, she really did—but every breath only inhaled his scent, that warm, heady scent that only came with hard work from a particularly delicious man. It overpowered her, sending tingles of anticipation for a kiss she knew she could not have roaring through her.

And words she would in any other situation have thought, let alone said, slipped out. "Well, you do not appear to be any cooler than when you started—though I admit, there have been times when I have wished to remove a few layers to keep cool."

Minny saw, she was sure, a flicker of longing. "I'm not stopping you."

It was all Minny could do not to throw herself into his arms. She would control herself!

Probably.

"Can I help you, by the way?"

Minny blinked. "I beg your pardon?"

Help her? The only help he could surely give her was the kind that whispered of tantalizing pleasure and a bed and—

"You left your stool and came over here," Henry pointed out, closing the gap between them to place himself a mere inch from her own body. "Did you...want anything?"

Minny swallowed. *Heaven help her from temptation.* Strike while the iron is hot? There would surely never be a situation more alluring than this!

But she had to stay calm—maintain what little dignity she had left.

"Oh, nothing from you," she said as airily as she could manage with lungs entirely devoid of breath. "No, I just—just wanted a hammer, that was all."

The rack of tools behind him was far too convenient. In any other situation, Minny would never have been tempted to do something so outrageously forward. But then, he had been the one to start taking off his clothes, hadn't he?

And it was not as though she was some fancy lady with a reputation to ruin...

Minny leaned forward, heart in her mouth. Her hand reached for the hammer behind Henry, and it was just complete chance that her hand brushed against his arm. It was scalding, or it scalded her.

A moan rumbled in his throat, and it was too late.

Minny gasped as Henry pulled her into his arms and kissed her, all her senses overwhelmed by him, and she did not care.

This was what she wanted.

She clung to him, one hand tangled in his hair and the other gripping his arm, pulling him closer. Nothing was close enough as his lips roughly parted hers and his tongue claimed her, pouring pleasure that made every part of her tingle.

Minny moaned, desperate for more as Henry responded, his hands tight on her waist.

Oh, it was heavenly, feeling the rough hair of his chest brushing against her! So intimate, the heat that poured between them, the heady knowledge that this was forbidden and yet so right!

Minny swiftly lost herself in the kiss, his tongue teasing sensual delights from her so swiftly, she was overwhelmed, head spinning, heart pounding.

"Minny," he murmured, pulling back only to trail warm wet kisses down her neck.

And all she could do was tilt her head back, safe in his arms, achingly longing for more yet not knowing what it could be.

"Henry, more," she gasped, her hands inexplicably drifting down his back and toward his buttocks.

He moaned as her fingers tightened. "God, I would give you everything, I—"

"Minny? Minny, is that you?"

Minny and Henry sprang apart as though burned. The voice just outside the forge was rough, full of the country lilt from the next village.

"Y-Yes?" Minny managed, astonished she was able to make any noise after such heady kisses.

Somehow Henry had released her, and it was agony to be apart. Not just the lack of his physical presence, which was pain in itself, but this ache within her now had nowhere to go, nothing to do.

Minny's eyes flickered to Henry who was hurriedly pulling his shirt on. His eyes danced with wickedness.

"Next time, I will have to make sure to lock the damned door," he breathed before stepping out of the forge and the kitchen.

And not a moment too soon. Mr. Chapman stepped into the smithy with a broad smile and his hat in his hands. "I thought I'd find you like this."

Minny tried to smile as she leaned back against the rack of tools, as though they would provide support for her frantically beating heart and quivering body.

"Like this?" she repeated.

Mr. Chapman nodded. "Here, in the forge. I wanted to talk to you about something, just a suggestion of course, but I think it will satisfy us both."

Minny blinked, trying to take in his words. *Satisfy her?* Nothing would ever satisfy her now other than knowing the taste of every inch of Henry Everleigh.

"Minny?"

She tried to laugh, though it echoed awkwardly. "I am so sorry, Mr. Chapman, I was momentarily—I was distracted, only for a moment, but you have come across me when I wasn't...suggestion?"

The farmer appeared nonplussed. *Clearly,* Minny thought dryly as her mind whirled, *Mr. Chapman considered women as nothing more than flighty things.*

"Yes, a suggestion," he continued blithely. "Well, I thought I have a number of horses that need shoeing, so I thought you could come over to the farm for a day—I'll send a cart if needs be—and that way..."

It was a good idea, even Minny had to admit. It was good business sense, good for her, and easier on the horses, too.

And she would give it some proper thought, the moment she could erase the memory of being held in Henry's scorching arms, receiving his scalding kisses.

CHAPTER ELEVEN

April 29, 1810

H ENRY HAD NEVER looked on anything more beautiful. It was perfection. It was…outstanding.

"*Voila!*" he said proudly, holding up his masterpiece.

The forge was unusually silent as Henry beamed at Minny who had been seated on the stool for the last hour or so, scribbling in that notebook of hers.

Ever since last week when he had lost all his senses and started stripping off before her—*not nearly enough, sadly*—Henry had been careful when working at the anvil when Minny was in the forge.

At least, he had tried to be careful. It was easier said than done, but in the following six days, he had managed *not* to kiss Minny senseless and admit his foolish scheme to identify a gossiping scandalmonger.

He had neither allowed the truth to slip through his lips nor permit his lips to lock on hers.

He should be congratulated.

Still. He was unusually aware of her presence whenever in the forge. Henry had been determined to focus on the task at hand—the task she had set him—and only twice had he lifted his head to take in the splendid beauty of her hair.

Well. Perhaps three times.

Yet despite that, he had managed to complete his first project at the anvil. And what a thing of beauty it was!

"Is…that it?" asked Minny faintly.

Henry's shoulders slumped. For some reason, there was neither amazement nor congratulations in Minny's tone. In fact, there was a strained smile across her cheeks and a puzzled expression on her brow.

Which did not make any sense. Why, he had never seen a horse shoe so splendid. Wiping beaded sweat from his brow, Henry gazed with delight at the curved metal in his hands.

It had taken him the best part of an hour, he would guess, and his shoulders ached.

"Remember," Minny had said only yesterday, "it's the detailed work that takes the time, that really puts the pressure on the nerves. When you have to take your time, if you want beauty to emerge."

Henry swallowed at the mere remembrance of her words. Yes, one had to go slowly if one wanted beauty to emerge. And he had tried to rush things, hadn't he?

Foolish cad, taking off his shirt like that! He would have to hope that never got back to the Dulverton Club. He would be eaten alive by his friends for doing such a foolhardy thing.

He had tried, since then, to tread more carefully. If he were going to get information from Minny—*and that was the only reason he was still here*, he tried to convince himself—he would need to go slowly.

And that was why his damned shoulder ached, and he'd forced himself to have cold baths every evening after returning to his room at the King's Head.

"What is it?" Minny said lightly.

Henry frowned. *Was it not obvious?* "A horse shoe."

It was ridiculous to be so proud, he knew. Part of his rational mind, buried deep under desire for Minny Banfield, could see the thing in his hand was nothing to write home about.

A curve of metal, poorly angled, not entirely smooth on one side.

Part of the metal had melted unexpectedly, and there seemed to be nothing he could do to fix it.

But still. It was, at thirty paces, recognizable as a horse shoe. Wasn't it?

"A horse shoe," repeated Minny in a level voice.

A prickle of irritation clutched around Henry's heart. He had felt such achievement, looking at it on the anvil, knowing he had created something from a mere lump of metal.

Just a month or two ago, he had not known one end of a hammer from the other!

Henry had been born and raised to be a duke. The Duke of Dulverton was not in the habit of using his hands for anything, save the ordering of good wine and the loving of women.

Which was why, in his mind, this was such an achievement. *After all*, Henry thought with a wry grin, *how many dukes could say that they had made something—anything?*

"It's definitely a horse shoe," he said defensively, still holding it up.

The spring sunlight glinted off the iron, throwing a glow around the forge.

Minny nodded sagely. "If you say it is."

"Minny!"

"Well, what do you want me to say?" she said seriously. "It is clearly an achievement for you, and I have no wish to detract from your enjoyment."

Henry allowed his hand to fall to his side, all excitement leaking away. *Was it truly that bad? Was it impossible to tell it was a—*

Only then did he notice the teasing smile on Minny's face. His loins lurched.

Dear God, she was a minx. What was he going to do with her?

More importantly, what was he going to do with himself?

"You are mocking me," Henry said, waving the horse shoe.

"Well, only a little bit," said Minny, eyes dancing with mischief.

"What did you want me to say?"

His heart thumped painfully as responses whirled through his mind.

Oh, I don't know, whispered his traitorous heart. *That you want me? That you need my touch, crave my attention, are just as conscious of where I am at all times as I am of you?*

That you want to be underneath me as I kiss your—

"It's just that I don't know any horses with feet like that," Minny continued, evidently unaware of licentious thoughts rushing through Henry's mind.

Henry took another look at the horse shoe. It was crooked, now he came to examine it closely, though his gaze shifted past it to the giggling woman.

Dear Lord, why had he thought her stern and stiff when he had first made her acquaintance? There was such joy in her, such heart.

And his heart yearned for it to be him, his presence, his kisses drawing it from her.

"Perhaps it will not perfectly fit a horse immediately," Henry conceded, trying to keep laughter from his own voice.

"Perhaps not," Minny said with a giggle. "Though I should not tease too much. Here, look at this."

Eager to accept any excuse to look more closely at the woman he was fast feeling too much for, Henry watched her step across the forge—leaving her notebook carefully closed on the stool.

His joy drained away. That notebook of hers, she was always writing in it, always scribbling away. Was it possible...Henry had come here for one reason, to find the person writing such terrible lies about his sister.

Was it possible that as he stood here sweltering, attempting to make his first horse shoe, his beloved sister was being slandered before his very eyes—by a woman who was becoming just as dear to him, although in a different manner?

Henry's jaw tightened as Minny rummaged in a wooden box

pulled from underneath a bench.

It was possible. He had never sneaked a look in her notebook, had considered it inappropriate.

But was his affection for Minny clouding his judgment? Was he risking a chance to find the miscreant...and was it possible that the miscreant was Minny herself?

"Here it is!" she said triumphantly.

Henry almost dropped his horse shoe onto the anvil in surprise. Minny was holding a lump of metal that looked like an iron bar bent in half. It was a horrendous lump of dross, really, but for some reason, she was holding it as though it were made of gold.

"And...what is it?" he ventured.

Minny's eyes glittered. "Why, the very first horse shoe I made, of course!"

She stepped over to show him, and Henry forced his gaze onto the useless lump of iron rather than the curve of her collarbone disappearing into the sleeve of her gown.

No good would come from it, he tried to tell himself. He was not here to bed innocent maidens. No matter how well they kissed.

"You are jesting me," Henry said aloud, taking the iron lump from her. "This is supposed to be a horse shoe?"

Minny tapped him lightly on the arm in a playful manner that almost forced Henry to forget all his stern promises and kiss her again. "It was my very first attempt!"

"So is this, yet it at least looks like the thing I was attempting to make!" Henry said with a laugh.

He held the two pieces of iron beside each other and immediately felt drastically better about his first try.

Minny raised a quizzical eyebrow. "Yes, but you are...what, five and twenty?"

Henry's stomach lurched. "Eight and twenty."

"And I was but seven years old when I made that," she said proudly, pointing to what she had called a horse shoe. "I was barely strong enough to lift the hammer!"

Blast. Henry had to admit, it was more impressive.

"I still win," he said aloud, permitting a teasing air into his voice.

Teasing was permitted. Standing close was acceptable. Dreaming of that soft skin under his fingers was—

"I suppose you have a little way to go, but so did I," said Minny, taking her horse shoe.

Henry's heart skipped a beat as her fingers brushed past his own. Had the forge suddenly grown much hotter?

"And you have time to improve," she continued, placing the keepsake back into the wooden box. "At least...how long are you planning on staying here, Henry?"

Henry swallowed. Her voice was nonchalant; she had not even bothered to turn around as she asked him the question. But perhaps that was the point. Perhaps she did not wish for him to see her face as she asked the question.

He certainly did not know how to answer.

"At least...how long are you planning on staying here, Henry?"

Perhaps he would have a better answer if he had managed to keep his attention on the task at hand.

Peg was at home—*or more likely,* Henry thought, *taking tea with one of her many friends*—and with every passing day, the damage to her reputation increased.

The longer he dwelt here with Minny in this strange dream of a life, the harder it would be to rectify the damage.

Yet, he could not drag himself away, look in her notebook, force himself to sneak about her kitchen and attempt to find any clues to prove whether she was a part of this mysterious plot to destroy his sister's life.

Henry's jaw tensed as Minny leaned against the bench, fixing him with a stare.

There was such beauty there. Such power, such strength.

He could also see pain, vulnerability, longing. He could see it so swiftly because it was a mere reflection of his own heart. What he was doing here was wrong. So why had nothing else felt so right?

"I...I don't know," Henry said hoarsely.

Forcing his scratchy throat to swallow made no difference. It was an important question; one he did not feel he could answer...yet she deserved to know he would not be staying long.

His very soul rebelled against the thought before Henry could speak it. *What, leave? Leave Minny?*

Admit his life was over and confine himself to dull bachelorhood?

"You don't know," Minny pressed gently.

Henry shook his head, as though that was sufficient.

"But your money will run out eventually, I suppose," she said quietly. "You cannot just stay here forever. You are not a gentleman, happy to lay about the place and do nothing!"

Her laugh was light, and Henry tried to laugh with her.

Yes. It was not as though he were a duke, with responsibilities back at Dulverton Manor. Not as though he had a sister depending on him. Not as though he could simply walk away from that life, title, prestige, and live in a smithy.

Tempting as it was. As she was.

"I have a little more coin laid aside," Henry said aloud, knowing it was an insufficient answer, but helpless to think of anything else to say. "I can stay a while longer. I mean, for the present. For a while."

God's teeth, his mouth was running away from him, but what was he supposed to do? Minny's eyes were bright, intrigued, and it was all Henry could do not to promise the world.

He was in deep. Too deep.

But his primary concern had to be Peggy. "I suppose at some point I will have to go to London to seek the next steps of my journey. I...have you ever been to London?"

There was a reason he had never been invited into the King's service. Subtle, he was not.

Yet he sparked a reaction—and one that made his heart sink.

Minny's cheeks flushed scarlet. "Why would you ask me that? What would possess you—London? Why London?"

"Only because—well, it's London. Everyone knows there are jobs in London," Henry said lamely.

The distance between them had opened into eons. Even if he gave into his wish to reach out and touch the woman swiftly capturing his heart, there was no way to reach her.

He had introduced a gulf between them, and it was one he could never cross.

Minny was frowning, suspicion across her face. "No, I have never been to London, and I don't know anyone who has been to London. I have no wish to go there!"

Henry's heart sank, if possible, even further. *Who was it that said the lady doth protest too much? Shakespeare? Marlow?*

"Ah," he said helplessly. "I see."

Minny glared, the ire he had seen when they had first met darkening her eyes. "Why do you want to know so much about London?"

"Oh, I don't know," Henry said helplessly, wishing to goodness it was late enough in the day to feign tiredness and disappear back to the King's Head.

But he had to try, didn't he? He could not retreat without truly trying. The information in London had said messages came back and forth from this very forge.

"One reads so many interesting things about London," he hazarded, keeping his eyes fixed on Minny. "In the newspapers. So much scandal, so much gossip."

Yes, there was no mistaking it. Her gaze flickered to the notebook on the stool, panic suffusing her face.

Henry's shoulders slumped. He should have known, should have kept focused, should not have allowed himself to be so easily swayed by a pretty woman and warm hands. Should not have kissed her twice.

Because she was a part of this. There was such guilt in her face, such fear, there was no mistaking it.

"I don't know what you mean," Minny said stiffly. "I have short shrift with those who meddle in gossip, they do not know what damage they can do to people's lives. They have no—their honor is—I have not read any London newspapers."

It could just be a coincidence, Henry thought wretchedly. His heart was traitorous, spirit weak, and he wanted so desperately for Minny to be innocent. A mere misunderstanding. Something they could laugh about one day, once he could unburden his heart to her.

And there was truth in her words, he could see that. Admittedly, Minny was also glaring fiercely as though she would fight him bodily if she had to, but nothing but honesty rang from her words.

"Right. Good—I mean, fine," Henry said hastily.

Minny waited, as though expecting a further attack. But that was his own imagination, surely. She could not possibly know what he was referring to. *Could she?*

"So," she said awkwardly. "What are you going to do with that?"

Henry blinked. *That? What on earth was she talking about?* "I beg your—what?"

"The horse shoe you made. The one in your hand," Minny said slowly, as though explaining something very simple to a very dense person. "You cannot possibly think to shoe a horse with it, I doubt any of the farmers around here would let you. So, what are you going to do with it?"

"Oh," said Henry blankly.

He looked at the cold metal in his hand. In his frantic thoughts about Pegs and Minny and scandal, he had quite forgotten about it.

There was no denying it would be a very sick horse to require such a horse shoe.

"I should melt it down, I suppose," he said quietly. "It can be no use to anyone."

Not unlike himself, Henry thought darkly. Here he was, a duke! Why had he not sent a servant to do this? Spying on Minny Banfield and discovering if she was connected to this mess should have been a task completed in a matter of days.

Yet he had lingered here, foolishly, slowly entrapping himself in emotions for the smithy's blacksmith he must fight...must, yet had not.

He was useless. A poor duke to permit such scandalous libel about his sister, and a poor blacksmith indeed.

A warm hand slipped into his. Henry started and saw to his astonishment that Minny had stepped across the forge and was smiling shyly.

They had kissed twice, once when his shirt had been most ridiculously removed. Yet, Henry found neither experience more intimate than this. Standing here with Minny's hand in his, in the place he was starting to think of as *their* forge.

"A thing is not useless if it is not perfect," Minny said quietly.

Henry's heart twisted. *Dear God, how did she manage to look straight into his heart?*

"It's special, because you made it. Why don't you send it to that sister of yours," she continued. "Show her what you have achieved since you set out here."

The thought of sending the terrible horse shoe to Peggy brought a smile to Henry's face. "I'm not sure whether she would appreciate it— but I know someone who would."

Minny raised an eyebrow.

"My friend, the d-devil of a friend," Henry corrected. *Hell, he almost said the Duke of Penshaw then!* "I think he'll appreciate my...talent."

His hand was gently squeezed. "Well. As long as someone does."

CHAPTER TWELVE

May 4, 1810

"—AND THERE—STRIKE WHILE the iron is hot!" Minny said cheerfully.

She almost snorted with laughter as Henry lunged as though the anvil was going to walk off if he was not swift.

"Like that?"

"Why not?" she said eventually, trying to keep the laughter from her voice.

Henry glanced over. "You are laughing at me!"

"You are dancing about like a fine lady," Minny teased. "As though you are worried the iron is going to get up and hit you back!"

For a moment, she thought she had gone too far. After their slightly prickly conversation last week—Minny had been certain he knew about her brother, testing to see if she would give him up—they had managed to settle into a routine that benefited them both.

In the mornings, Minny would conduct all business required. Sowing season was over and many ploughs had come into the forge for repair, and there had even been a commission from the manor for a new set of tongs. That had been worth more than ten shillings.

But by the afternoon, there was usually not much to do. That was when Henry took over at the anvil.

At least, Minny thought to herself with glee, *he thought he took over.*

There was not much that got past her, even as she sat here on the stool.

"I don't hit it like that!" Henry protested, eyes wide. "At least...I don't think so. Don't I?"

Minny's heart softened. "You do."

Why did those words make her flush? It was bad enough that she no longer seemed able to look at him merely as a handsome man.

If she were forced to explain it—*to her brother, most likely*, Minny thought wryly—she would say there was something about Henry that went beyond mere looks. Something deeper. Refined in a way she had never expected in someone not a gentleman, yet a gentleness, too.

Oh, he was a puzzle. The trouble was, Minny knew she was definitely not supposed to unravel him.

"It's cold now," she pointed out to force her mind away from such wild thoughts.

Henry looked aghast. "Oh, blow!"

"There is no better time to strike when the iron is hot," Minny said with a shake of her head. "Now, you can heat it up or you can—"

"Put it aside and bank down the fire."

She blinked. That was not the response she had been expecting. "What?"

Most inexplicably, Henry was pulling off the heavy leather apron her father had left her and folding it carefully. The iron on the anvil was being carefully ignored—something her father would never have approved of—and the furnace was indeed being left to smolder.

What did he think he was doing?

"I'm putting it aside," Henry repeated, head tilted. "When was the last time you left the forge, Minny?"

Her heart fluttered as she heard her name on his lips. "Left the forge?"

How did he do this to her? Reduce her to a mere automaton who could do nothing but repeat the last words spoken?

There was a much too knowing glint in his eye. "Yes, left the forge."

Minny tried to think. "Well, I went to see Mr. Chapman about—"

"I don't mean on smithy business. I mean actually left the forge and the work behind. Did something else."

"You know perfectly well I have not done that since you arrived!" she said in astonishment. "Where would I go? What would I do? When the fire here needs tending—"

"No, it does not," Henry said firmly.

Minny forced herself to close her mouth rather than look like a total nincompoop. How was Henry to continue his work with the iron—one day, he had assured her, he would create a horse shoe a horse could actually wear—if the fire went out?

He fixed her with a firm gaze. "The work's done, and my shoulders ache. You need to stretch your legs and think about something that isn't the forge, Minny. Come on. Let's go for a walk."

"But...but..." Minny spluttered as Henry stepped around the anvil and offered his arm. She took it without knowing why. "But I can't—"

"You have finished your work for today, is that right?" Henry asked smoothly as he led her out of the forge.

Minny blinked in the afternoon sun. Summer was still a little while away, but after spending so much time in the dark forge, it was dazzlingly bright.

"Minny?"

"Well, yes, all the work is—"

"And you don't need to lock up, or something, do you?"

She snorted. "Lock up? Here in Pathstow?"

"Excellent," said Henry triumphantly, as though she had wandered straight into his trap. "In that case, there is no need to linger. Off we go on a walk."

And he marched forward with her hand in his arm, pulling her forward.

Minny almost stumbled as they walked along the street. Why, she could not recall the last time she…a walk? That was the sort of thing ladies and gentlemen of leisure indulged in. They had nowhere to be, no work to complete, no money to earn.

Their money earned itself, Minny thought darkly, though she was at a loss to know how.

When she had to go somewhere, there was no fine carriage to transport her or elegant mare to ride. She'd had to depend on her two feet and walked as fast as she could to reach her destination in the quickest time.

Which was what made this so…unusual.

"What are we doing?" Minny hissed under her breath.

Henry's laugh was felt through her shoulder as well as heard. "Just walking, Minny! Have you never been on a walk before?"

Well, of course she had! Except…except not like this. Not as though they had no care in the world. As though nothing could divest them of their happiness.

Her stomach twisted. If they were going to go on a walk, the phrase uncomfortable, they could at least go somewhere they wouldn't be gawked at.

"There's a market in Pathstow today," Minny said quietly. "Come on. The footpath."

It wasn't really a footpath, more a forgotten track that had somehow escaped the enclosure. Minny had always loved Pathstow Common, where her parents and their parents had grazed their animals. Though it was partially enclosed now, there was still a way across it that meandered beautifully along a stream.

"Oh, how picturesque!" Henry exclaimed.

Minny giggled. "I'm sorry, what?"

"I mean, how nice," he corrected hastily.

She shook her head but said no more. It was not his fault, she supposed, that sometimes he sounded like a lord with an iron bar shoved up his—

"So, I suppose that is where the saying comes from," Henry said conversationally.

The wind gently ruffled Minny's hair as she looked curiously at him. "Saying?"

"Strike while the iron is hot," he said. "I always thought it was something to do with the way Jenks ironed my—I mean, the way gentlemen had their collars starched."

Minny frowned. "Who is Jenks?"

Was it her imagination, or did Henry look discomforted? *There was so much she did not know about him, after all,* she thought wretchedly. Even the little snippets he let slip were usually followed by something that hid the real truth.

"Jenks is…is a manservant to a duke," Henry said quietly as they turned a corner, heather blowing in the breeze. "He irons shirts and collars, that sort of thing."

Minny laughed. "Goodness, what a terrible life!"

Had Henry's arm stiffened? "Why do you say that?"

"Well, one's time is never one's own, is it?" she said, wondering why on earth he could not see the obvious. "I mean, he is always at the beck and call of his master, I suppose. Unless he is fortunate, I imagine the duke is an absolute bore."

"He's not—"

"How well do you know a duke?" Minny asked curiously.

She was not imagining this time. Henry's expression clammed up immediately, and he looked away at the horizon.

His gaze lingered there as he said vaguely, "Oh, more than I would like. And then sometimes I realize, not at all."

It was all nonsense as far as Minny was concerned, but the sun was shining and the wind made her feel more alive. Perhaps it was the company.

"Well, I think the phrase comes from blacksmithing," Minny said aloud, as though the rather awkward exchange had never occurred. "Striking when the iron is cold is a waste of time, naturally, and so striking when the iron is hot—"

"—is best," Henry finished with a nod.

His gaze had drifted to the stream which fed the Pathstow well. A pair of ducks quacked angrily for disturbing their peace as a heron flapped its wings and decided there were better places to fish.

"And so in life, too, I suppose."

Heat seared Minny's cheeks. Henry's words were spoken wistfully, as though there was a great regret on his heart that he could not speak of.

What could a man like this regret? What opportunity had he missed, perhaps, or ignored entirely because he simply did not strike while the iron was hot?

Minny nodded, not trusting her voice as they meandered slowly alongside the stream.

He'll be leaving soon.

The thought crossed her mind before she could stop it, and it hurt.

Once he had learned how to make a horse shoe properly, Minny was sure, he would be gone. What else could he possibly have to stay for? His curiosity would be sated, and he would disappear off to London, to that place of gossip and scandal, without a backward glance.

Who would want to stay here, in Pathstow, in the middle of nowhere with naught but the gossip of a small community to entertain?

Minny's throat hurt as she swallowed. It was her home; she could conceive of no other. It was foolishness to even consider going with him…

"And what about you?"

Minny started. Henry's warm smile caused ripples of affection—affection she should certainly not be feeling.

"What?" she said hastily.

Henry shrugged. "I just wondered whether you...well. Regret not striking, if you know what I mean."

Minny narrowed her eyes. "We're not talking about iron anymore, are we?"

There was a strange tension in the air. She could feel it flowing from him and into her as they continued along the common, not a single other person in view.

These were dangerous questions with dangerous answers, Minny knew. She would be a fool to answer them honestly. But the idea of lying to Henry...

"No," she said. "Yes. Perhaps. It is difficult to tell, in hindsight...I do not know."

Her cheeks were surely dark red as she looked at the mud splattered hem of her gown.

"I do not know."

That, at least, was the truth. Did not know what to do with all these feelings bundled up in her heart. Did not know if these feelings rushing through her could be trusted. Did not know if similar emotions raged in the heart of the man beside her...

Her gaze was pulled inexorably as though a connection already existed between them.

Minny found Henry's eyes staring deep into her own, and there was a moment—just a moment.

A moment they shared that seemed to speak, albeit silently, of the passion they both felt but both knew they could not express. Not without scandal. Not without crossing lines of decorum. Not without irrevocably changing their lives.

Minny swallowed. "I—yes, I had the chance to do something, once. Something else."

"Not blacksmithing?"

She shook her head.

"But you did not take it?" Henry's voice was curious, something

Minny rarely experienced in the opposite sex.

Why, the last time her brother had been truly interested in a part of her life, she thought darkly, *it was because he wanted to ask her to set up this network.* Information passing back and forth from—

"Why not?"

He looked at her closely, as though he could tell the answer just by sight. Minny grasped at the chance—the excuse, really—to look back at him with just such an intensity.

A graze of stubble across his cheeks. A freckle, just in the corner of his eye; unless one was very close, one would miss it. The strength of his arms, yes, but the softness of his hands. The gentleness of his lips as they tugged into a smile.

"I suppose it was something rather tempting."

More tempting than you? Minny wanted to say. Instead, she blurted out the first thing that came into her head, the truth. "No, I almost was married."

Henry came to an abrupt stop, halting so swiftly Minny jerked her hand out of his arm, the momentum carried her forward.

As she turned to him, ask whether he had a stone in his shoe or seen something, she realized a look of absolute horror had clouded his face.

"Married?" Henry said menacingly.

Minny nodded, unable to speak. What could she say? He had spat the word like a malediction, as though she had committed some great offense.

And truly, it would have been, if she had agreed to marry him. But she had not. And besides, that was over a year before Henry had ever—

"Married—you, married?" Henry repeated. "How—why would you even think of—you received an offer, then?"

Minny swallowed, hating how eagerly she wished to console him with the full facts. She should not think of him that way. If Mr. Henry

Everleigh had wished to marry her, he'd had plenty of opportunity to ask such a question since he started learning the ways of blacksmithing in her forge.

So why was he looking at her like...like she was a possession? Like he owned her, the very thought of another man touching her an outrage?

Minny knew she should be offended. That did not prevent a spark of pleasure.

"Yes, I received an offer," she said quietly, wishing she could have her hand tucked into his arm again. There was something so comforting about his close presence. Besides, it was cold now she was without him. "From Mr. Chapman, as it happened, but—"

"The blaggard!"

"Henry!" Minny breathed, shocked.

But not as shocked, clearly, as Henry himself. He brought a hand to his face to hide his expression for a moment, his fingers gripping at his temples as though he had received devastating news.

Why did Henry treat this as...as well, Minny could think of no other explanation other than a betrayal!

The wind blew harder, tugging at her hair. A chill rushed through her. "Henry, I—"

"From Chapman!"

"I do not see why you are so angry about it," she shot back, her temper flaring as she knew it would. "It was before you and I ever met, and it is not as though—no promises have—I do not understand why this vexes you so heartily!"

And that was when Henry slowly lowered his hand to reveal his face.

Minny gasped. The truth was painted so clearly on his face that he had no need to speak. He cared.

That he was attracted to her was no great surprise. Minny had attempted to memorize every single moment of those two kisses they had—wrongly, of course—indulged in. Was it not possible he had done the same?

But what she saw in Henry's expression was more than mere desire. It was longing. Affection.

"You know why," Henry said quietly, not taking his eyes from hers. "You know exactly why."

Minny shivered, though the movement had nothing to do with the temperature of Pathstow Common.

Oh, this was a mistake. Had she not already seen what heartbreak did to a person? Was she not fully aware of the traps of affection when unreturned, unrequited, or forbidden?

"It…it would have just been a marriage of convenience," Minny breathed, taking a step closer to Henry as though to console him. "I could not have married him."

"But he did ask you," Henry said quietly. "And you could have said yes."

"Yes, I suppose I could have done. But I did not. I…well. I wanted a little more spark in my life than Mr. Chapman could offer."

She had somehow managed to stand far closer to Henry than she had intended. Her breasts rose heavily as she struggled for breath, and the fabric of her gown brushed up against the linen of his shirt.

Was that a moan? Was that from her throat or his?

"Minny," Henry breathed.

Minny leaned toward him as his hand cupped her cheek. Oh, she wanted nothing more than to be in his arms again, to throw all caution to the wind and to declare she loved—

"I think I should go."

Minny lowered her head, her forehead touching his own. It was wonderful, standing here with Henry so close, his forehead pressed up against hers in a moment of such intimacy. She was astonished she was still standing.

"I know," she whispered. "But I wish you wouldn't."

It was the most she could permit herself to say. She felt the shudder of aching desire in Henry before he spoke.

"I know, but I think I have to," Henry said darkly. "Or I'll...I won't risk your reputation, Minny. Not out here."

The hint of a promise of what could be shared in privacy flittered across Minny's mind as she tried to focus on this moment, this closeness, this intimacy that would at any moment—

Henry stepped back. "You will not mind, of course, if I do not accompany you back to the forge?"

The forced stiffness in his voice was more painful than the words themselves, but Minny forced herself to smile. What she wanted, what she hoped for...it was impossible.

"Of course," she said brightly. "I will see you tomorrow."

Chapter Thirteen

May 7, 1810

EVERY INCH OF Henry's shoulders ached, but he did not stop. Once he stopped, he would have to see Minny. And then he would have to tell her…

The swing of the ax tore at his muscles as it sliced through the log. The two halves slowly toppled off the stump outside the blacksmith's. The noise of the forge, the anvil being tapped twice as Minny worked, the hit echoing around her garden.

Henry bit his lip. He should go in, really. He had chopped enough logs in the last hour to last Minny a lifetime.

Well. Perhaps a month.

But with every passing moment he put off the inevitable, even as the sun started to wend its way slowly toward the horizon. It was touching it now, just kissing the hills in the distance.

Yet still Henry did not go into the forge.

"You're a damned fool," he muttered, rubbing his thumb on his shirt in an absent way.

There was a scrape across it—not quite as bad as the time he had whacked it with the hammer, but still. His thumb hurt. It appeared to be getting continuously injured, and there did not seem to be much he could do about it.

Like his heart.

Henry grimaced as he leaned down to pick up the two halves of the log and threw them onto the pile. Perhaps a few more logs, before he went in. Before he told Minny what he had decided last night.

It had been a talk with Ted, of all people, which had decided it. Henry had walked into the King's Head with a smile on his face and his heart singing.

Just to be close to Minny was a gift, but with each passing day he was certain he was getting more intimate. Parts of her were opening up to him he had never guessed could be there, and it made him feel…

Everything.

"You look well, sir," Ted had remarked as Henry had approached the hatch for his customary evening pie.

And Henry had grinned like the fool that he was. "I am well, sir!"

Ted's eyebrow had raised. "And so you'll be staying in Pathstow for good, then?"

And all the happiness had drained away. Henry had stared, aghast. "Stay? Forever?"

The thought had never occurred to him.

At least, when it did, it was pushed aside immediately and replaced with the far superior "take Minny away from this place and ravish her in every bedchamber in Dulverton Manor". Of which there were many.

But the idea of actually staying here in this pokey little village…*there was nothing wrong with it*, Henry had thought, his stomach squirming. But it was not the place for a duke. The Duke of Dulverton could not bury himself here!

"Well, you seem to be getting along well with Minny," Ted had said affably, clearly unaware of the turmoil he had unleashed within his guest. "And you've been here two months. More than enough time to know if a person is…well. Right for you, if you get my drift."

Henry's look of horror had transformed into a look of outrage. "I beg your pardon?"

His voice was stiff but his heart was thundering painfully in his chest. What on earth had he done? Evidently, he had given the whole village to understand he would be marrying Minny—a blacksmith!

Three months ago he would have laughed at the very suggestion. He wasn't laughing now. Was that what she believed? Did she expect some sort of proposal in time, in short shrift?

"I won't risk your reputation, Minny. Not out here."

And Henry's jaw had tightened. He could stay no longer. Not to give Minny high hopes for something that could surely never occur. A duke, marry a blacksmith? Marry any woman who had not been raised suitably, brought out into Society with the best of chaperones?

No, it was unheard of. Unthinkable!

"Sir?"

And besides, Henry had thought frantically, Peg had been left on her own for too long. It was not fair for her to be forced to navigate the wiles and dangers of Society without him. He was her brother; she depended on him.

How else would she know when to accept the proposal of a gentleman?

"I said, sir?"

And worst of all, and Henry's stomach turned most violently at the thought, he still needed to track down the gossiping liars spreading those rumors about his sister.

It was certainly not Minny. Why, he had spent all day with her, every day, for almost two months. Not a single sign or hint had she given that she was in any way mixed up in this.

Wretched though the thought was, he no longer had any reason to stay in Pathstow. With Minny.

"Sir!"

Henry had started and glowered at Ted for interrupting his thoughts. "What!"

"I said, do you want a little porter to take upstairs with your pie, sir," the ever patient Ted had said.

And he had. And that whole night, Henry thought darkly as he heaved the ax over his head and chopped another log in two, he had been unable to rest.

Something was warring within him that he could not control and never would have predicted. A desire…to stay.

Foolishness, Henry told himself as he placed the two halves onto the log pile. The sort of foolishness one would expect from a young man entering Society, instantly taken with the first lady he saw.

Not a man like himself, grown, and wise, not at all easily swayed by a pretty face.

The memory of how Minny had laughed at him only that morning for thinking that the wheel rim she was mending had been a crown soared into his mind. A lopsided grin tilted Henry's face as his stomach lurched and his heart beat fit to bursting.

He was in danger here. He had seen it coming and yet done nothing about it.

He needed to leave. Return to Dulverton Manor, or better still, London—for Peg was there—and continue his search for the blaggards ruining her reputation.

Henry sighed. So why was he still here, putting off the inevitable break with Minny, chopping logs?

Shadows had grown longer as he had been lost in his thoughts, the sun halfway disappeared. It would be night soon. Sighing heavily, Henry picked up what he promised himself would be the final log and placed it on the stump.

"Henry!"

He whirled around, his instincts so strong that he dropped the ax with little thought to his toes and rushed toward the kitchen.

Minny. She had called him, and though he knew it was ridiculous, he could do naught but answer that call.

"Minny?" Henry said as he stepped through into the forge.

There she was. Tired after a long day of work, Henry noticed, affection pouring through his veins. Yet just as beautiful as when they had first met. Perhaps more so. Was that normal—to discover with each passing day that the beauty of one you cared for deepened, blossomed, shone more brightly?

"Can you help me with this?" Minny said, not looking around as she leaned over the anvil, hammer in her hand, furnace blazing. "A hammer, grab it will you?"

A smile crept across Henry's face as he reached for one of the hammers, carefully hung up on the rack in order of size.

She had expected him to come. She had called, and he had appeared. Why was there such beauty and elegance in that?

"Here, take a look at this," Minny said without looking up.

Henry approached the anvil as one would approach an altar. And was it not the same? Did not transformations occur here that went beyond faith? Was it not glorious to see Minny here, in her element? Cheeks pink, sweat beaded on her brow, her gown mostly covered by the thick leather apron that hid so much and yet suggested—

"Henry?"

"Yes, yes, right," Henry said hastily.

That was the trouble with being around Minny in a forge, he thought ruefully. One was inclined to lose all sense of why one was here. *And get burnt.*

He looked at the anvil. There upon it lay a candlestick, glowing red. After weeks seeing Minny at work in the forge, he could easily see what she was doing.

"You're mending that candlestick," he said helpfully, as though she did not know.

Minny glanced up. "Well done. Are you able to help me with it?"

Henry's stomach lurched as the heat of the candlestick started to warm him. That had to be it, didn't it? It couldn't be that he was so flattered by Minny's request for help that he—

"Henry!"

"Yes, yes, I'll help," Henry said with a dry laugh. "Sorry, I was just looking at...what do you want me to do?"

"Tap here, just a few inches beyond—yes, that's right. Two on the anvil, a gentle one on the—now a little harder..."

Minny was an excellent teacher. There was nothing more infuriating, Henry had always found, with someone who was attempting to impart knowledge but who did it in a confusing manner.

His fencing tutor, Caelfall, had always been like that. No patience for the learner.

But Minny was different. Standing shoulder to shoulder with her, trying not to think about the warmth of her skin against his as their arms brushed up against each other, Henry carefully followed her instructions.

Joy soared through his chest as he saw their combined work, slowly, mend the candle-stick.

Time seemed to have disappeared. He could have stood there forever, Minny instructing him, the warmth of the forge nothing to the warmth pooling in his loins.

Because Henry knew, somewhere deep inside him...that this was it. The last time.

"There!" Minny exclaimed before lifting the candlestick and placing it back in the furnace, shaking it to really thrust it into the coals. "Well done."

Henry absolutely glowed. To an outsider, perhaps, they'd assume that was because of the warmth of the place. But he knew it was different. Though he would not speak the words aloud, though they felt strange even to think them, Henry knew as he watched Minny fondly just what had happened.

He had fallen in love like an idiot.

Well, Henry thought as he drew himself up and placed the hammer back in its place on the rack, *he would soon fall out of love.* The moment he returned to London, he was sure, he would forget about her and—

"Thank you, Henry," Minny said softly as she placed the candlestick gently into the cold water. It fizzed wildly during her next words. "I could not have done it without you."

And that was when Henry realized, with a painful renting agony in his heart, that he wouldn't. Forget her. Forget Minny? He could sooner forget his own name.

She was a part of him now, his whole life twisting tack the moment he had met her. That scowling suspicion she had cast on him had melted away in the heat of the forge and all that was left was affection.

That was, Henry reminded himself, *on his side*. True, Minny had accepted his kisses, but that did necessarily mean that...well. He would be a fool to assume it. He would be an even greater fool to do anything about. Not with him leaving tomorrow—

"You did good work there, you know," Minny said with a weary sigh, untying her leather apron and pulling it off. "Very good."

"I would not be able to do such good work unless I had an excellent teacher."

Blast. Was this what "telling her he had to leave" looked like?

He needed to get a grip on himself, and fast, or he would find completely different words slipping from his tongue, and that would be...unfortunate.

Minny Banfield may not know he was the Duke of Dulverton, but he was still a man. He had no wish to excite expectations he could not fulfill. More than he had already.

"Well, I would say that's us done for the day," Minny said cheerfully. "I'll probably do a stew tonight, if you want to stay."

"If you want to stay."

Sweet agony bellowed through Henry's chest. Stay? Oh, he wanted nothing more than to stay. Leave behind the rules and responsibilities of being a duke—though bring with him some money, of course—and stay here with Minny. Be with her.

But he couldn't. Henry tried his best to push the thought away, but the desire—for it was a desire, far more than a passing thought—refused to cease.

If he could just ask her...

"M-Minny," Henry said, discovering to his surprise that he was breathless.

Minny stepped around the anvil. "Y-Yes?"

Henry swallowed. Oh, he was sure there were words. Somewhere, someone would find the perfect way to say this, but it was not him.

I have to go. I need to leave. My sister—my family needs me. My title requires...no, probably not that one.

All words seeped away when he looked into the wide and trusting eyes of Minny Banfield. He craved her as he had wanted nothing else, and she was a mere inch away.

Ready to be taken.

"Henry?" Minny breathed, her fingers somehow tangling in his own. "What do you want?"

Henry almost groaned but managed to stop himself. The sun had gone now, leaving them in the dark glow of the dying furnace.

They were alone. It was expected now that he would spend a few evenings each week dining with Minny; he would not be missed at the King's Head. He could stay here all night...

"What do I—"

"Want, yes," Minny said quietly. He could feel her pulse through her fingers. It matched the frantic beating of his own. "What do you want, Henry?"

Everything. All of you, forever, to stay here and—"I need to go."

The words had slipped out before he could stop them, and Henry saw in horror she was astonished to hear such a blunt statement.

Minny's fingers slipped away. "You—you must be tired. The King's Head—"

"No, not to the King's Head," Henry said wretchedly, hating that she took a step back, hating the distance between them. "London. I need—I have to return to London."

A look of deep disappointment clouded Minny's face. Henry hated it, but hated even more than she swiftly turned away, took a deep breath, then turned back to face him with an evidently forced smile.

Oh God, she did not want him to know how deeply she was hurt. That fact cut through his chest like a knife.

"Why?"

"And it's not as though I have been that useful here, not really, you will manage perfectly well on your own," Henry said in a rush, unable to stop himself. Perhaps if he kept talking, the pain in his heart would go. "You did excellently without me, after all, and—"

"Henry—"

"And I've chopped a great deal of wood for you, and I will fetch more water if you wish it tomorrow morning," he continued, raging against the agony that was driving them apart.

But it was his agony, wasn't it? His choice?

Minny was staring as though she had never seen him before and that was perhaps what broke him the most. "Why are you leaving, Henry?"

"My...my sister needs me," Henry said helplessly. "And you don't."

Well, it wasn't a complete lie, was it? From some angles, it was the truth.

Peggy could not be permitted to endure the scandal she was undoubtedly weathering on her own, and Minny...he had never met a more capable woman.

Henry could not help it; he reached out and took Minny's hand in his own. "You don't need me," he said quietly, "and that hurts, Minny, and don't ask me to explain it because I can't, but—"

"I need you."

"—and if you ever need help, I will give you an address you can—what did you just say?"

Henry's chest tightened as he held his breath, mouth agape.

Minny's cheeks were flushed but her expression was bold as she looked up with an air of determination and vulnerability. "I need you, Henry," she said softly.

She could not mean it. He was dreaming—

"And if you don't kiss me right this moment," Minny said with a mischievous look. "I shall have to kiss you."

Henry pulled her into his arms and clung to her, his embrace one of relief and uncertainty. What came after this he did not know—but he did not need to.

He had Minny in his arms.

She twisted in his embrace, turning her face toward him, and Henry eagerly claimed her lips with a moan. This was where he belonged. How could he even think about going? Pegs could fend for herself. She had Lady Romeril on her side—and he needed Minny.

Sparks of pleasure roared through him as Henry's hands clasped Minny's buttocks and pulled her close, as close as he could manage. She responded fiercely, kissing him more boldly than she ever had done, demanding pleasure.

And he was all too happy to give it.

But then she pulled away. Still standing in his arms but refusing to give her lips to him, Minny laughed as Henry groaned and tried to kiss her again.

"Minny—"

"Henry Everleigh," she said firmly. "I don't want you to leave. Not yet. I've shared so much with you—"

"I know, and I'm grateful for the lessons you've—"

"Not that," Minny said with a wicked smile. "I don't want you to leave, you hear me? Not until...we've shared everything."

CHAPTER FOURTEEN

"*I* DON'T WANT *you to leave, you hear me? Not until...we've shared everything.*"

Minny swallowed, looking into the eyes of the man she adored.

And why shouldn't she? Why shouldn't she kiss him, say such things, invite dishonor upon herself? It would all be worth it, to be with Henry...

She could feel his fingers pressed up against her buttocks, each one a brand, marking her forever. For she would never be able to kiss anyone else, could she?

Not now that she knew the taste of Henry Everleigh. No one else would ever match him. Henry had somehow crept into her heart so slowly she had not really noticed it happen.

Oh, the kisses had helped, Minny thought with a twist of pleasure around her center. But this was new.

This wasn't just attraction, it was...something more. She had never known there could be more, but Henry had awakened things in her...

"Shared...shared everything?" Henry repeated blankly. "I...I don't know what—"

Minny tried to prevent her nerves from showing. *It was natural,* she told herself, *to feel...worried about this.*

It was the first time she had ever considered such a thing, after all, and many in her situation would consider what she was about to suggest absolutely outrageous!

She might have done, if it were not Henry Everleigh. But he wanted to leave her.

"London. I need—I have to return to London."

Minny could not wrap her head around it. Why would Henry wish to leave, just as they were settling into such a wonderful pattern of joy and contentment? Perhaps even more?

"I don't want you to leave," Minny said firmly, though her boldness shocked even her. "Henry I—there was a man once who left, and I did not say anything because I was afraid, and I have always regretted—"

She felt the change in him before he spoke. Henry stiffened, his hands slipping from her as his eyes narrowed.

"Another man?"

At once Minny realized her mistake. A nervous laugh escaped. "I did not mean—"

"You said before old Chapman proposed matrimony to you," Henry said, his voice dark. "Dear God, are you honestly trying to tell me now, of all moments, that you regret—"

"No!" Minny placed a hand on his chest and felt the thunderous pounding of his heart.

In a way, it calmed her own. Here they were, standing in her forge, the one place she always felt safe—with the first person ever to make her feel truly safe and unsafe at the same time.

"No, you have misunderstood—I have not explained this very well!"

Henry glowered. "No, you have not."

Minny took a deep breath. It wasn't a betrayal, not really. She was not giving the whole story, after all, and surely, he would never begrudge her sharing his tale if it were to bring her to happiness.

Alan would have to forgive her.

Henry was still glaring. "Minny, if you don't explain—"

"It was my brother," she said in a rush.

They were still standing together, Minny in his arms, and she felt the softening of his grip as he relaxed.

"Brother?"

Minny nodded. Oh, she should have told him days ago, weeks perhaps—but then, Alan had always made her promise she would never reveal anything about him to others. It was too dangerous. The notes she sent proved that.

But she needed Henry to understand. That meant telling the tale.

"My brother was…was hounded out of this village," Minny said quietly, swallowing as she recalled that awful time. "I tried to stand by him, but I never properly—I should have asked him to stay, told him we could face it all together."

Curiosity flittered across Henry's face. "Why was he—"

"That doesn't matter," she said hastily.

She had promised she would never tell. Even Henry's warm kisses could not drag that particular secret from her.

"My point is, I did not strike while the iron was hot," Minny said ruefully, smiling at the look of dawning comprehension on Henry's face. "I knew what I wanted, knew I had to speak up if I wanted it…but I didn't. So I'm doing that now."

Henry's hands lightly clasped her waist. "You…want me to stay?"

Minny nodded slowly. A growing need for him had been creeping over her so gradually, it was hard to pinpoint precisely when the hammer had dropped and she had fallen completely in love with him.

But she was. She loved Henry Everleigh, and if his response to the mere suggestion of Mr. Chapman was anything to go by, he cared for her, too.

Which was undoubtedly why the words she should say were somehow replaced with, "I don't just want you to stay here, in Pathstow. I want you to stay here with me…tonight."

Henry stared, his eyes widening.

Heat tinged Minny's cheeks; it was a bold suggestion indeed, but she could not just let him leave without knowing how she felt about him. Without knowing how deeply she was attracted to him.

It was strange, one never thought about ladies being attracted to their lovers. Minny flushed as she thought of the few times she had discussed such things with her mother. It had always been gentlemen—or men—who had uncontrollable urges.

But this growing need was clamoring for attention, and if Henry did not kiss her—

"You cannot mean that," Henry breathed.

Yet he did not give her any time to respond. His lips had already met hers, and Minny moaned in his mouth, the connection so sweet.

Everything in her leapt at his touch, anticipation tingling across her skin. The ache in her was growing, building, hotter than a furnace and fueled differently, but she would not let those flames go out.

Not now she had leapt for her chance to have the man she loved.

"I mean it," Minny gasped between kisses. "And I think you want—"

"Oh Minny, you cannot even imagine what I want," Henry growled.

His ardor was so passionate, the candlestick they had mended together slipped to the floor with a clang. Minny ignored it. She could make new ones, but this moment with Henry was something she could never recreate again.

The first time they truly allowed their passion to blaze.

"Oh!" Minny gulped as Henry pushed her back toward the anvil.

It was a relief to find it was cold to the touch. Her buttocks pressed against it, Minny reveled in the sensation of being trapped between it and the hard presence of Henry's chest.

Her fingers were tangled in his hair, but just as she was about to claim another kiss, Henry's hands left her.

"Henry?"

Minny blinked. Her vision had become hazy thanks to her passion and the gloom of the forge, but as her eyes continued to adjust to the light—or lack thereof—her mouth fell open.

Henry was slowly unbuttoning his shirt. "I cannot tell you how much I wanted—"

"Yes," breathed Minny, reaching forward.

Her palm splayed across his chest, the dark hair she had seen that one time when he worked at the forge without his shirt under her fingertips. It was an image which had plagued her dreams ever since.

A lump rose in Minny's throat as she became overwhelmed by desire and confusion.

Once she stepped over this line, there was no way back.

"You have to be sure," breathed Henry, as though he had read her thoughts. "Truly sure, Minny, that this is what you want."

Minny hesitated. It was so easy to be swept away by feelings like this, wasn't it? At least, that was what she was discovering.

But as her eyes met his, the certainty she had been lacking flooded into her chest. She wanted him.

"I want you, Henry," Minny breathed. "Henry!"

His name had escaped her throat in a shout of surprise as his hands lifted her bodily from the ground and placed her on the anvil itself.

The metal was cold through her gown, but it was nothing to the heat roaring through her body. Minny watched with desire-hazed eyes and a certain amount of confusion as Henry took a step back and then slowly, ever so slowly, started to lift her skirts.

Minny swallowed. The brush of his fingers against her ankles—for of course, working in a forge, she wore no stockings—was causing tingles of sensual delight all across her body.

"Henry, what are you—"

"Trust me," Henry breathed as he gently pushed her skirts above her knees. "You can tell me to stop anytime you want, do you understand?"

Minny nodded, her voice unable to speak. *Oh, she had never—no man had ever—*

"Beautiful," Henry whispered.

Heat rushed through Minny as Henry gently parted her knees as her skirts reached her hips. She was exposed as never before, but there was no look of revulsion in his eyes.

No, quite to the contrary.

"Henry, I—Henry Everleigh!"

Minny had been unable to help it. Grabbing the anvil with both hands and arching her back as the sensations overwhelmed her, her eyes fluttered shut as Henry leaned forward and kissed her thigh very gently.

"Do you want me to stop?"

"No," quavered Minny, holding onto the anvil for dear life as Henry's teasing kisses moved upward, dancing along her thigh until he reached—"Oh, God!"

He was kissing her on her secret place. More than kisses, his tongue was darting over her, along her, then into her as Minny was overpowered with pleasure.

And Henry was moaning, as though he was enjoying himself!

Minny recalled the look of delight and desire that had flashed in Henry's eyes as he had beheld her, and gave herself up to the pleasure. The anvil was broad enough to hold her as she quivered, the delightful ache in her building as Henry's tongue licked and sucked until—

"Henry!"

Minny had been unable to help herself. His name was cried from her lips as ecstasy dazed her, a cresting heat that blazed through her in a rush of tingling frenzy and unknowable pleasure.

Henry did not cease his kissing until Minny's body went limp and she fell back across the anvil.

She could not tell precisely how much time had passed before she opened her eyes, still lying back on the anvil. It was to see Henry's face above her, delighted but with concern creasing his forehead.

"Did I truly please you?"

Minny swallowed twice to bring a little moisture to her mouth. "Please me?"

"I tried to—"

"You tried very well," she managed, heat searing her cheeks at the disgraceful nature of their conversation.

But then, if she could be taken to such fiery ecstasy on her own anvil, perhaps she should not be so shy as to talk about it.

"I want you, Minny—all of you," Henry said quietly, his hands resting on her thighs, his fingers stroking her, teasing even more pleasure from the fireball which had already erupted within her. "I can take precautions, but you need to decide—"

"Oh, yes," Minny murmured.

More pleasure? More ecstasy? More opportunities to touch and be touched?

Henry groaned and his hands left her.

His absence was like the closing of the furnace door, an abrupt and rather unpleasant sudden loss of heat. Minny looked up, desperate for him, then whimpered with the expectation of pleasure at the sight her eyes took in.

Henry was fumbling—rather poorly, it had to be said—with the buttons of his breeches. Eventually his patience ran out and he tore the things down, revealing—

Minny swallowed. She had known, in theory, of course. One could not live in the country and be completely unaware of the facts of life. The farmyards around the place were full of them.

But she had not expected…well.

"I want you to get you ready for me," Henry said in a jagged voice.

Minny almost laughed. "I do not think I could be more—oh!"

Perhaps she could. Henry's clever fingers were gently rubbing over her, and as she laid back and accepted the adoration, pleasure sparking across her body as she squirmed, he groaned.

"Christ alive, you're ready."

"I want more, Henry," Minny gasped, trying to describe the ache within her. "More of you, more, please."

Henry bit his lip as he nodded, pushing aside her knees to stand between her thighs. "You are—Minny, you have to know, I think I love—"

"Oh God!" Minny could not help it.

He had pushed himself, just the head of his manhood within her, and the sensation was overwhelming. Far greater than his tongue throbbing with his withheld passion, Minny felt herself slowly increase to permit more and more of him.

The slick movement twisted at something deep within her, and Minny whimpered.

Henry immediately halted. "Minny, are you—"

"More," she gasped, clinging onto the anvil as she remained on her back, adoring the way they were slowly becoming one. "There's a—a fire in me, Henry, and I need you to—"

"Minny," Henry moaned as he thrust deeper into her, sheathing himself completely.

It was everything she wanted and more, and Minny knew she would never be the same again. How could anyone be the same after something like this?

"You are incredible," Henry murmured as he thrust into her again.

Minny whimpered. Oh, this was too much—the way he spoke, the way he touched her, the way they had thrown all caution to the wind and abandoned all sense and reason—

"So beautiful," he continued, his hands on her hips as his thrusts grew in both depth and pace. "Every part of you makes me want to—"

"Yes," Minny moaned, his words driving her beyond all endurance, her eyes fluttering open because she wanted to see him as he ravished her. "Yes, more—"

Henry swore under his breath. His thrusts became rhythmic, forceful, taking everything from her yet giving everything in return. "Minny, damn, you make me—"

"Yes, yes," she whispered, the ache growing inside her as the heat he built started to rage. "Yes, yes, yes!"

This time she had no time to twist her lips around his name. The rush of fiery pleasure roared through her body, making every part of her tense and quiver, and Minny gave herself to the flames.

"Minny!"

Something had evidently happened in Henry, too, though Minny was not entirely sure what. His thrusts became pounds as he poured himself into her, his breath sharp, gasps echoing around the forge as he clung to her hips for dear life.

Minny let go of the anvil and moved her hands to his own, clasping them tightly as they shared the pinnacle of pleasure, waves roaring through them.

She would never know anything like this with anyone else—and she had no wish to.

Henry Everleigh. A man with no prestigious name, no reputation, only a little money…and she had given herself to him.

"Damn, woman, you took everything from me."

Minny smiled, a wickedness she had never known until Henry had introduced her to such pleasure. "Does that mean in a few minutes you will be unable to go again?"

CHAPTER FIFTEEN

May 8, 1810

T RY AS HE might, Henry had never grown accustomed to the uncomfortable bed at the King's Head.

That was the trouble, he supposed, of growing up with down mattresses, eiderdowns of the softest goose feathers, and pillows stuffed with the softest gander feathers. Even as a child, only the very best for the future Duke of Dulverton.

Since becoming the duke, of course, his beds had only become more resplendent. Velvet coverings embroidered with gold silk covered even larger beds. Large enough for him to stretch out like a starfish and not quite reach the corners.

No wonder he had struggled to sleep in the poxy single bed tucked into a dark corner of the room at the inn.

It was why Henry was astonished, upon waking in Minny's arms, to discover three things.

Firstly, he had slept well—the best night's sleep, perhaps, since leaving Dulverton Manor in a fit of pique after discovering someone in Pathstow was the gossip monger.

Secondly, he never wished to sleep anywhere else other than with Minny in his arms.

And thirdly, most surprisingly, that he loved Minny with a dark and dangerous passion that meant he would be incomplete without her.

Sunlight drifted through the thin curtains of her bedchamber window. He hardly remembered how they had got up here—his memory too overcome by their passion, his skin tingling with recalled pleasure.

The sheets were softer than he would have predicted, perhaps a sign of how his heart had softened. Besides, it was Minny's skin, not sheets, that brushed against his.

Henry turned slowly until he was looking at Minny.

Dark eyelashes grazed over her skin, fluttering as she dreamed. Her breathing was slow, her breasts moving under the cotton nightgown she had eventually flung on after declaring, at a godawful time in the early hours, she could no longer take any more pleasure.

Henry swallowed, his heart pattering painfully. He could spend a lifetime attempting to understand this firebrand of a blacksmith and still never uncover all her complexities.

Minny Banfield.

The only trouble now, of course, was understanding precisely what he was going to do with her—with himself. Do with these feelings Henry had tried to deny for weeks.

But after sharing such passion with her, how could he pretend his desires for Minny were wholly innocent?

A slow smile spread across Henry's face. No, he would not describe what they had shared together last night as…innocent.

Minny shifted in her sleep. Henry held his breath as though that alone could prevent her from waking. A cockerel crowed. The sound of a cart, slow and steady with the clopping of a horse ahead, echoed around the small bedchamber.

Pathstow was waking up. It was only a matter of time before someone arrived at the forge. The least he could do was get the furnace going.

He was out of practice, however, at sneaking out of bedchambers and leaving the bed's occupant undisturbed. He grasped at his clothes, pulling on breeches and shirt without any incident. Though he was able to pull the cover back onto the bed without disturbing her, the moment he stepped across the room—

"Henry?"

Henry turned as his heart melted. Minny had opened her sleep-filled eyes and blinked in the daylight.

"Morning, Minny," Henry said softly. "I'm going to get the furnace going."

She stared as though he had started spouting Hindustani, then her gaze sharpened as she took in his words. "I will help—"

"You will stay in bed and enjoy the first slow morning in you have undoubtedly experienced in a good long while," Henry said firmly, a wry grin slipping onto his lips. "Rest."

But Minny was pushing herself up in the bed. "No, I must—"

"Must nothing," Henry said, putting his hands on his hips and raising a sardonic eyebrow. "Do you mean to tell me you have absolutely no desire to sit in bed with the luxury of knowing your man is doing the dirtiest and most difficult job?"

Minny's cheeks flushed crimson, but she did not drop her gaze. "My man?"

Henry swallowed. *Well, it was a little presumptuous.* No promises had been made between them, no offer—as though he could offer!

Not that he didn't want to offer. Damn. But a duke and a black-smith—she did not even know he was—

"I rather like the sound of that," Minny said dreamily, slipping back into the pillows and fixing him with a languid look. "My man."

Henry's heart skipped a beat. He liked it, too. *Blast.* He would have to think about this later—in this moment, he needed to step out of the bedchamber before his manhood started to do the thinking for him and he ravished her again.

"Furnace," he said shortly, as though to remind himself precisely what he was supposed to be doing. His fingers itched to reach forward, remove that nightgown and—

"Glad to hear it," Minny yawned. "Goodness, I cannot recall the last time I just stayed in bed, it feels…wrong, somehow."

Henry resisted the urge to tell her that when living as the Duke of Dulverton, it would be a fine day indeed that he was out of bed and dressed before midday.

"I am sure it does, but I urge you to rest, Minny," he said aloud. "I'll even allow resting out of bed, if you truly do not do any work. You hear me?"

The smile she gave him was so dazzling, it threatened to melt him into a red-hot puddle, much like her furnace downstairs could. Henry did not understand it. He was no fool—at least, he did not think so. Yet standing here, feeling the biggest fool in Christendom.

"Rest," he repeated as though that would break the spell she somehow had over him. He took another step back. "Rest!"

Minny giggled as Henry opened the door and closed it behind him, leaning against it for a moment as he caught his breath.

It was a wonder he had not got down on bended knee and offered himself, all his wealth, and the duchy to boot. A woman like that…

Something he would have to untangle in the privacy of his room at the King's Head, once today was over.

Henry's mind rebelled against the idea as he stepped into the passage alongside the forge. *Back at the King's Head?* How was he supposed to sleep in that pokey room, when he knew there were welcoming, soft arms waiting for him here?

Swallowing hard and hoping to goodness the hard work ahead of him would distract him, Henry strode along the passage and into the forge.

It was freezing, as was to be expected. Heaving a heavy sigh, Henry allowed his muscles to take over. The routine of stacking the furnace, choosing the best logs, putting them carefully in place, layering small logs, coals, and kindling took over.

There was a sort of pleasure in the activity. Henry would never have believed it if someone had tried to tell him before he had arrived at Pathstow, but the knowledge of doing something productive, following a routine, knowing this went here and that went there…

There was something calming about it, if that was the right word.

That was perhaps why at first, Henry did not notice the sound of shifting feet above him. Only when he first lit the furnace and started blowing the bellows rhythmically did he realize what his ears had been trying to tell him for a few minutes.

Minny was up and about.

Henry rolled his eyes. *It was almost impossible to keep that woman still!*

Her muffled footsteps sounded down the stairs and into the passage. Henry had rather expected—hoped—she would come straight into the forge. Despite all his fine words about her resting, every moment he was not looking at her felt, somehow, like a moment wasted.

But she did not appear.

Henry paused for a moment at the bellows, curious. If she were not coming into the forge, then she was surely going into the kitchen. But there was no sound of footsteps in the room next door.

A flash of dark, almost black hair.

The windows in the forge were small, like most windows in the village, but Henry's eyes were so attuned to Minny, he immediately spotted her movement from the corner of his eye.

Something stirred in his stomach. *She was outside?* What could she possibly be outside for?

Placing the bellows on the anvil and telling himself he was allowing the furnace to settle, Henry stepped soundlessly across the forge and peered out of the window.

His heart skipped a beat and joy rushed through him. There she was. His Minny. In the growing brilliance of the sunshine, she glowed almost like an angel—an angel, that is, that made his loins stir and every part of wish to throw aside his title and spend his life here, with her.

Henry swallowed. *Why, she would make a remarkable duchess.*

The thought pattered through his heart at almost the same moment Minny did something most unaccountable.

She looked around, as though reassuring herself she was alone. Her eyes glazed over the forge windows, and Henry's heartbeat increased at the idea of seeing something he should not. Something forbidden.

Then she pulled something from her nightgown pocket. Something small and pale and folded into a square. *A letter?*

Henry's stomach dropped as he watched the woman he loved place the folded letter into a place behind the water trough, wedging it in so tight it was impossible to see it was there unless one had watched it be placed there.

And then she rose, smiled briefly, and stepped around the smithy toward the door.

Henry reached a hand to the wall to steady himself. His legs were shaking, his whole mind reeling at what he had just seen.

He had been right all along.

"No. Believe it or not, the miscreant who I will be dealing with is…the blacksmith."

Dear God, he had never wished to be so wrong before, but he had been right. Every moment he had been here, Minny was merely waiting for a chance to sneak out and place one of her scandalous, gossiping, reputation-ruining letters out for her partner.

The room spun. Henry blinked several times, but his vision did not calm.

Minny? Minny Banfield?

That she could do such a thing, spread gossip most heinous and painful! Surely she must know the consequences of her actions, must know that what she did harmed not only the women she wrote of, but their families.

How could she write such slanderous gossip? The woman Henry knew—or at least, the woman he thought he knew—would never wish to harm another.

So why was it so easy for her to write in that damned notebook, he realized with increasing horror, the sorts of headlines which had potentially soured all suitors for his sister?

"Henry, I thought we could…Henry?"

Henry turned slowly on the spot, hoping to goodness the world would stop spinning. It did so the moment his gaze fell on Minny.

She was standing in the doorway with a swiftly fading smile. A shawl was wrapped around her shoulders, her nightgown still the only thing she was wearing. If Henry had not been so horrified at what he had just seen, he would have taken the opportunity to strip off the nightgown and worship the body of the woman he…

But how could he even countenance the thought of such a thing now?

"Henry? You look awfully strange," Minny said quietly. "What—"

"You," Henry said softly.

It was clear she had no idea what he meant, or the wild pained thoughts whirling through his mind.

How could he have been so stupid? How had he managed to let his lust, his desire for seduction overcome his better nature—his care of his sister?

Henry swallowed. *Oh God, Peg.* All that she had suffered the last few months, it was his fault! He'd come to Pathstow to root out the truth, and he'd permitted the scandal to continue right under his nose.

"Henry, you're frightening me," Minny said softly, stepping toward him. "What—"

"You. It was you. You, all along," said Henry darkly. He raised an accusing finger. "You're the one that's been sending the secret messages!"

Minny halted and stood staring, clutching her shawl around her as though the forge was cold.

But he had done a good job at laying the fire, Henry thought. It did not quite make up for the terrible job he had done in looking after his sister, but he did know how to build a fire.

If only he knew how to dampen the fire roaring through him. Love, passion, pain, anger, it all burned within him, feeding off each other as shame pointed out just how easily he had been tricked.

"All this time, I thought it would be someone using the forge to drop off and pick up messages," said Henry bleakly. "I—I looked out for anyone who was coming here frequently, looked for the person I was sure was guilty but—"

"But you found me," said Minny quietly. "Are you shocked?"

Henry wanted to fall to his knees and beg her to recant, to say she did not mean it, that it was all a misunderstanding.

Lady Margaret Everleigh shocks ton by meeting secretly with lover

Lady Margaret Everleigh suspected to be with child

Hushed up Dulverton scandal rocks Society...

Each one of those sordid headlines...had been born here.

"You did not stop to think what gossip could occur from your writings?" Henry asked with a dry throat. "You did not consider, for a single moment, what would happen when those notes of yours reached London?"

She blanched, turning away as she spoke. "I did what I thought was right."

"Was *right!*"

Henry had not intended to shout, but it appeared she was going to leave him no choice. It was an outrage! Where was the principled and honorable woman he had come to care for?

Where was the woman with whom he had thought he could share...

Well, all thoughts of that nature would have to be completely ended, Henry told himself fiercely. His heart raged, pulse pounding with hot fury, but he could not tangle his tongue around the words that he knew he had to say.

That she had, although unknowingly, betrayed him.

"And would it shock you to learn, Miss Banfield, that your letters have already damaged, perhaps beyond repair, the reputation of someone dear to me?"

Minny's face whipped around. "I did not know you were acquainted with—"

"I am," Henry said bluntly. *How could she look at him so calmly?* "Your betrayal—"

"My betrayal?" She stepped forward, just as much fury on her face as Henry imagined was on his own. "I did not do this to betray others, but to share information vital to—"

"How could you possibly think such information was vital!"

Words swirled around Henry's memory, words that had brought Peggy's social standing down to that of a mere servant!

...the Lady Margaret has no honor left...

He closed his eyes for a moment as though that would cease the rush of pain circling his mind, but it was no good.

He had come here to find a cad. A brigand. To find the cur destroying his sister's life with unfounded gossip. And all he had managed to do was fall in love.

"The notes don't hurt anyone," Minny was saying. Henry's eyes snapped open as she continued, "I feel passionately—"

"Oh, yes, I am sure you do," Henry snapped. "How much were you paid, eh? How many lives ruined because of what you did—why, for all you know, the life of a duke himself may have been impacted!"

The impression of his words were not precisely what he had hoped.

Minny snorted and rolled her eyes. "I doubt very much there is a duke in the world who even knows I exist!"

And he should have held his tongue, but he could not help but say—"You're wrong, I know you far better than any other man on this earth!"

He was hot, far too hot. Henry did not understand it, he had barely moved in the forge—but it was growing in heat as his own anger grew in temperature.

Minny stared, mouth open. "Y-You know—but you're no duke!"

Henry pulled himself together and tried to throw out his chest in the imperious way he had been taught as a child. This was it. Once he uttered these words, there was no going back.

How could he, now he knew it was thanks to Minny Banfield that his sister's prospects for matrimony were essentially over?

"My name is Henry Everleigh, Duke of Dulverton," he said impressively, his voice carrying around the forge. "And I will never forgive you, Minny Banfield, for what you have done."

Minny stared as though she had never seen him before. Pain flickered in her eyes.

Most unaccountably, as far as Henry was concerned. She was not the one who had been wronged. She was the one profiteering off the demise of others. She had lied, kept secrets, broken his heart—

There was only one thing this pain in his chest could be, wasn't it? His heart ached, broken under the pressure of the discovery.

"I was right," Henry said as though holding onto that fact would provide sanity. "I knew it was coming from here. I knew the smithy had something to do with—"

"You're a duke?" Minny interrupted, her voice cracking. "A duke—you lied to me all that time, came to me under false pretenses, and you believe what *I* have done to be wrong?"

Just for a moment, Henry could have forgiven all if she had dropped into his arms and wept and told him she regretted it. That perhaps she had been goaded into it, did not know the import of what she did.

But hearing those words, he knew it was over. Whatever they had shared, whatever he had...had hoped could be.

"You scoundrel," he said quietly. "You miser. You cruel harpy— you villain!"

His sister Peggy swam before his eyes as Minny opened her mouth in shock.

"I return to London immediately," Henry said stiffly, striding past her and out of the forge. "Expect to hear from my lawyers."

He did not look back. Not even as he heard the door slam and after it, a sob.

CHAPTER SIXTEEN

I T TOOK MINNY but five seconds for the anger to cool into pure
liquid rage.

"I return to London immediately. Expect to hear from my lawyers."

The—the audacity! How dare the man speak to her like that—if he
even was a duke, which she doubted.

The door she had momentarily slammed opened again and Minny
stepped through it, every step crackling with anger.

She was not going to permit any man, let alone one who had
done…done *that* to her on her very own anvil just yesterday, speak to
her like that!

The figure of Henry Everleigh—*or*, Minny thought darkly, *his royal
dukeness, or whatever she was supposed to call him*—had not traveled far
down the street. In fact, it only took five paces to grab his collar and
start dragging him back to the forge.

"Hell's bells, what the—Minny!"

"Save your breath," Minny said menacingly. "This conversation is
not finished."

Henry tried to twist out of her grip, but she was not going to make
it that easy for him. Years of working in the forge had given her great
strength in her fingers, and Minny was rather delighted, in truth, to
find she was more than a match for the struggling man.

Man? Gentleman. Duke.

Dear Lord, this was going to get complicated.

Still, there was simplicity in the small things. Like, for example, how satisfying it was to thrust Henry into the forge and slam the door.

Minny leaned against it and looked at the man who only last night she had thought...

Well. If he could shout such things at her, if he was against the works he was doing, then he was not a man she wished to be associated with.

Nonetheless, she thought wildly as she glared at the man who stepped toward her as though to intimate her into getting out of the way, *she would have her moment.* Henry had spoken over her, not given her any opportunity to explain.

"Let me out, you fool," snapped Henry.

"I am no fool, and I am not going to permit you to leave my presence until I have had my say," Minny returned with just as much vehemence. "You think—"

"I think precisely what anyone else would think—that what you do is abominable, unacceptable in polite Society!"

Minny laughed bitterly. "Oh yes, I know what I do is not accepted by polite Society, but my convictions tell me—"

"Your convictions must be torrid indeed if you believe what you do worthy!" Henry snapped.

Minny stared. *This was outrageous!* She performed a service, a great service. Had she not risked her life, several times, to ensure the messages her brother needed to share were passed on? Though the world may condemn them, she would not betray them, nor accept she did anything wrong in helping them.

"What I do is honorable," she said, jutting out her chin and looking into the fierce gaze of a man who, just an hour ago, had adored her. "Even knowing your disdain for me, I would do it again in a heart—"

"I don't need to listen to this," Henry said, turning toward the kitchen.

Minny was not sure what made her do it. Perhaps it was the righteous anger rushing through her veins, or the sardonic way he spoke to her. Perhaps it was the wild sense that he had lied to her, lied about who he was. Perhaps it was the sense their conversation had been unequal and she was due her turn to explain.

Whatever it was, it spurred Minny on to shout, "You would uncover my brother and end his life?"

The words rang about the forge. She hated them, hated she'd had to say them—but she had no choice.

Henry halted. He turned slowly and examined her for a moment before saying, "There is no death sentence I am aware of for spreading rumors and lies."

Minny blinked. *Rumors and*—"What on earth are you talking about?"

The last few minutes rushed through her mind swiftly as she attempted to discern what on earth the man—the duke could be talking of. Rumors and lies? Why, the only messages she had shared or passed on were those of love. What could the man be thinking?

"I am speaking," Henry said slowly, as though she was both hard of hearing and hard of thinking, "of the messages you are sending to London about my sister!"

The words hung in the air. Minny waited for them to make sense, but no matter how long she paused, they did not. "Your...your sister?"

Henry nodded abruptly. "Yes."

"But..." Minny tried to collect herself, tried to understand this misunderstanding.

Sister? She had never heard of an Everleigh before Henry—and given the nature of the notes she passed on, the likelihood of them even *mentioning* a woman...

"I...I have absolutely no idea what you are talking about," Minny said helplessly, shrugging. "Why would I write about your sister?"

"Because gossip about Lady Margaret Everleigh is lucrative, of course!" Henry growled. "Because her ruined reputation in the gossip columns of London newspapers undoubtedly sells them, and it is my duty to save that reputation!"

Minny stared at him.

Sister? Gossip columns?

Only then did understanding start to dawn, slowly, in her mind.

He thought she was part of some sort of gossip mongers. Oh, dear Lord, how had they managed to get this so tangled?

Minny swallowed as she recalled what Henry had hurled at her mere moments ago.

"You scoundrel. You miser. You cruel harpy—you villain!"

He had it all wrong. But he had not trusted her, believed her, thought of her well enough to doubt for a second that she could be entangled in such a horrendous scheme.

Minny took in a deep breath. Well, whatever she had hoped could be between her and Henry Everleigh was over. She could see that now. He was so swift to believe the very worst of her, how could she believe the best in him?

But she would not permit him to return to London with a false impression. That he would have to leave was not in question. Minny could not bear the thought of him staying at Pathstow, not now they had shared so much. Not now she knew he was a duke.

Not after she revealed what she was about to tell him...

"Henry Everleigh, if you had taken more than five minutes to consider who I am and what I am, you would have realized I would never have been part of such a despicable thing as to slander your sister," she said evenly. "You dolt."

The lack of fury in her words took the wind out of Henry's sails. His shoulders slumped as his eyes widened. "You...you haven't...you aren't—"

"If you had bothered to give me the respect of even half your brain," Minny continued, ice cold stiffness in her tones, "I may have explained to you, right there and then, what I was doing."

Henry took a step forward. It barely closed the gap between them, but it shot a bolt of panic up Minny's spine.

If he got too close, she was not sure she would be able to hold to her convictions and stay out of his embrace…

"You haven't been spreading lies and gossip about my sister?"

Minny snorted. "Not in the slightest. What do I care about the reputation of Lady Everleigh?"

"Margaret."

"Whatever!"

"But then…" Henry took another step closer, and Minny hoped to goodness her resolve would hold. "Then what have you been doing? For you cannot deny you have been sending messages, Minny."

Minny fixed a glare upon him. "Miss Banfield."

She watched him swallow, recalibrate everything he thought he knew about her for the second time that morning. Oh, it was such a muddle—yet he had brought it upon himself. If he had just believed in her goodness…

"Miss Banfield," Henry said quietly. "What have you been you doing?"

Minny's heart flickered painfully. She had promised Alan she would never reveal his secret…but surely this was one occasion beyond the norm.

No one could ever have predicted a duke would arrive at Pathstow, pretend to be naught but a man, and work with her in the forge…

"Minny?"

Minny swallowed. *She had come too far now.* "I am part of a network that passes on messages between men."

Henry raised an eyebrow. "Is that all?"

Irritation sparked through her heart. "No, that is not all! 'Tis a dangerous job doing what I do, for the men who are part of this network are…are men who love men."

There. It was said.

Henry stood there waiting as though expecting further words. When it became clear she was going to speak no more, Minny watched as his mind started to put the words together.

His face fell. "Oh."

"Oh, indeed," Minny said dryly.

Dear God, it was as though she had admitted she was working for the French! There was incredulity on the man's face, his handsome features sagging as he tried to understand.

"Y-You mean—"

"Yes, I mean," snapped Minny. "Goodness, one would think you had never met a molly before!"

"But I—I haven't!" Henry spluttered. "At least, I have heard of such men, but—"

Minny could not help it. A snort of laughter, dark and mirthless, escaped her lips. "You know, you probably have. You just probably did not realize. It is rare for a molly to reveal himself unless in the presence of friends. True friends."

Though she wished to drop her gaze, she managed to hold Henry's as she spoke. She was not ashamed.

"But then you mean that you are acquainted with—"

"My brother," said Minny, hoping to goodness she would be able to warn him before the duke returned to London. "And my father, I think, though of course there were some things a parent would never share with a child."

That had done it. Henry's jaw fell open, his astonishment escaping in a medley of laughter, choking, and spluttering. "B-But that doesn't—can't imagine what—you're sure?"

Minny sighed as she leaned against the door. The anger which had propelled her into this conversation was spent now the words were spoken.

All she had done for her brother, the messages between him and his lover she had shared, the news of raids in Brighton, London, Wells she had warned men of...the loyalty they had shown each other, the affection deeper than what she had seen in the marriages around her.

And here was Henry Everleigh, astonished a man could find affection in the arms of another man.

"Am I sure love between two people is always precious, always to be trusted and defended?" Minny asked quietly. "Am I sure I have done all I can to help and protect those who have no help nor protection under law?"

Perhaps something of her quelled anger showed in her tone, or perhaps it was in her face, for Henry dropped his gaze.

"You cannot know what it is to love and see danger in every opportunity to reveal that love," Minny said, her voice soft. "I saw it in my brother. He adored...well, it is perhaps best not to say. Once the village found out, that was it. He was forced to leave, to forfeit all opportunity to take up the forge. And when I saw how swiftly I could help those who loved contrary to what the law dictates, I am not ashamed to say I have taken every opportunity to do so."

For a moment, she was certain Henry was going to chastise her. Critique her perhaps, for loving men who were so different to what Society expected.

So, when he eventually spoke in a low voice, his words were a shock. "I am sorry."

Minny blinked. She must have misheard. "I—I beg your pardon?"

"I did not know—"

"Of course you did not, because you did not have the decency to ask," Minny cut across him.

Her heart still thumped wildly, but there was a sick pain in her stomach that would not cease. No number of apologies could undo the words he had hurled.

"You scoundrel. You miser. You cruel harpy—you villain!"

The man she had thought she knew, had loved, was a dream. Just that, a dream.

Henry Everleigh was a man who judged first, shouted first, then did not even think to ask questions later. He was dangerous. He was fiery, much like her, but Minny always believed she directed her passions to good.

And what had Henry done? Accused her of something she had never done, against someone she had never even heard of, then stormed out.

"Minny—"

"Miss Banfield," she corrected sharply. She glared, trying to make him understand. "You came here, to my home, to my forge—"

"I only wanted to—I thought—"

"You thought wrong," Minny snapped. "Dear God, I thought I was doing you a favor!"

Something shifted in Henry's gaze. "I was paying you."

"Nothing more than I earned, the amount of time I wasted with you!" Minny did not believe the words she shouted, but the pain in her chest had to be purged somehow.

He had shouted at her, hadn't he? He had believed she was capable of cruelty, of gossip, of the desire to end a woman's reputation. Well, perhaps it was time he heard a few home truths of his own.

"You," Minny said quietly, taking a step forward. "You were so convinced of your superiority in intellect and understanding, you did not hesitate to consider whether you could have the complete wrong end of the stick."

"Minny, I—"

"And when you did, you were swift to censure me," she continued, glaring as she took another step forward, hating her frantically beating heart. "I, a woman on my own, without protection—"

"I would never have—"

"You were going to set your lawyers on me!"

Henry had the good grace to look awkward. "Yes, but...dash it all,

Minny, I thought you would understand! You did what you did for your sibling, and that was precisely what I was doing!"

"And would it shock you to learn, Miss Banfield, that your letters have already damaged, perhaps beyond repair, the reputation of someone dear to me?"

But it was too late. Minny could no longer look at him and see the man who had become so dear over the last few weeks.

Instead, there was only a man who disbelieved all the goodness he purported to find in her, who was swift to declaim her as a harpy, and who believed the best way to deal with such a disagreement was to send lawyers against a woman.

No, it was over.

"I am sorry, Minny—"

"Miss Banfield," Minny repeated, emphasizing each syllable. "Mr. Everleigh—or your highness, or whatever you need to be called! You believed the worst of me. You called me a harpy!"

She watched him wince. Then—

"It's Your Grace, actually."

And there it was. The anger which had flared, then died down, flared again as though the bellows of her soul were pumped harder than ever before.

Minny blinked away the spots that appeared in her vision as she did her best not to fly at the man. That was the trouble with a temper like hers. It was always about to be let loose at the most inconvenient—

"Get out."

Henry blinked. Then he stepped forward, and Minny found to her horror he was now mere inches away. She could not help but breathe in the heady intoxication of his scent. She could feel his warmth. Only a few inches separated them, and it was impossible not to feel the pull she had been unable to fight yesterday.

The desire she felt for him.

The passion she knew he could swiftly awaken in her.

All she had to do, Minny thought wildly, *was lean forward.* Her lips would touch his, and all her principles, all her determination to do what was right, would melt away.

Melt into his arms.

"I am sorry, Miss Banfield," Henry breathed, his gaze flickering from her lips to her eyes. "I was wrong—entirely mistaken. I should not have said—"

"No, you should not," said Minny, trying to keep a hold of herself. "But you did."

Her eyes filled with tears. Oh, if only he could take back those words, if only he could erase them from her memory. It would be as though he had never accused her, merely waking that morning in each other's arms and deciding to be happy for the rest of their lives.

"Once said, those words can never be unsaid," Minny whispered, heart breaking.

"Minny—"

"I would be grateful if you would depart from my forge and my home," she said, whipping away from him before all self-control was lost.

It was only a few steps to the door but it felt like an age. At every moment, Minny was certain Henry would reach for her, grab her hand, pull her back—and a small part of her wanted him to.

Wanted him to kiss away the hurt he had hurled at her just moments ago.

But that touch never came. Instead, Minny felt the cold iron of the doorhandle between her fingertips as she twisted the knob and opened the door.

Pathstow appeared. A new day. Villagers were meandering toward North Street where that week's market stalls were being erected. She could hear complaints of the weather drifting on the breeze.

"Minny, I—"

"I don't want to hear it," lied Minny, glaring at the man to whom she had given everything. "Please leave, Your Grace. I got it right that time, didn't I?"

She had worked hard to keep all warmth from her voice, and it appeared she was successful. For the second time that day, the Duke of Dulverton strode out of her forge—but this time, Minny did not race after him.

She closed the door slowly, turned to lean against it, gently slid onto the floor, and allowed the tears she had fought for so long to burn down her cheeks.

CHAPTER SEVENTEEN

May 11, 1810

HENRY LEANED WEARILY against the impressive front door as it slammed behind him.

There. He was home. He had reached the Dulverton family town-house in London, and only just before midnight, too.

Everything ached—but it was not the ache of shoulders and back-side after several hours in a godforsaken coach, bumping over the rough roads and cobbled streets between here and Pathstow.

No, it went deeper than that. Henry shrugged off his greatcoat and handed it wordlessly to the footman who appeared at his side. *Dear God, he had missed servants.*

"I'll take a little supper in the drawing room," he said quietly. "I have no wish to disturb Lady Margaret, I am sure she went to sleep hours ago—"

"Lady Margaret is…um…"

Henry blinked. It was unlike the Dulverton servants to contradict their master, but it was even rarer to hear a tone of uncertainty in their voices.

Trying to summon all the energy lost when he had confronted Minny on her deceit—erroneously, as it turned out—Henry fixed his gaze on the unfortunate servant.

The footman shuffled his feet, fingers tightening around his master's greatcoat. "It is just—Lady Margaret is not abed."

Henry waited for further details, but none it appeared were forthcoming. "Not abed."

The footman shook his head.

Only then did a noise interrupt their conversation.

It was a giggle. A laugh, high pitched, almost certainly his sister's. But what on earth was Peg doing up at this time of night—and she was clearly not alone, for a dark hum of a masculine voice murmured after her laugh.

Henry's stomach churned. *What on God's name was going on?*

"Supper, in the drawing room," he snapped as he strode to the drawing room door.

"Your Grace, I wouldn't—"

Henry threw open the door. The sight of his drawing room swiftly met his eyes. A well-proportioned room, elegant by day and refined with the curtains pulled and candles lit.

There was also a fire in the grate, which was most astonishing at this hour. There were two glasses of wine, almost empty, on a console table near the large sofa. And there, on the other side of the room, standing breathlessly and with wide eyes, was his sister.

"Peggy," Henry said, closing the door and stepping forward. "What in God's name are you—"

"Nothing," she said swiftly.

Henry's eyes narrowed. "Pegs."

His sister flushed. Now he came to think, her cheeks were already flushed, but they darkened as he said her name.

It was most strange. *Peg had always been one for early nights,* Henry thought wildly, famous for it in the family. Why, there were evenings when it would not be possible to keep Peg from going upstairs to bed before nine o'clock!

Yet here she was, the clocks of the house chiming midnight, and she was awake!

"Where on earth have you been?" Peg said defiantly. "You've been gone for months, and half of London is talking about it."

Henry winced. *Damn.* That was precisely the opposite of what he had intended, but it couldn't be helped now.

He had sufficiently burnt the bridge that had taken him from London. There would be no reason to go back there, not after what he had said to Minny.

"You scoundrel. You miser. You cruel harpy—you villain!"

"Henry?"

"Peg," Henry said heavily, sitting on the sofa and lifting the glass. "Thank you for procuring the wine, I don't know how you knew I would be home today."

His sister smiled weakly. "Yes. Yes, the wine—the wine is for you."

Henry nodded as he picked up the bottle. That was one of the things he loved about his sister—she was so thoughtful. The poor thing did not deserve to have such slander...

He lowered the bottle, then raised it again. "Don't tell me you've drunk all of this?"

His sister's eyes snapped to the bottle, then back to him. "No."

Henry hesitated. *Two wine glasses.* "Peg, you weren't..."

The thought was distasteful before he spoke it—and he must be mistaken. There was no possibility that his sister was entertaining a gentleman?

No, if Henry had learned anything, it was that when he made assumptions and acted rashly, he was the one to be made a fool of, ending up on his ear feeling wretched about the whole thing.

Pushing the suggestion of what could have occurred to one side of his mind, Henry poured himself a large glass and drowned the wine in one gulp.

The heat of the red wine seared his throat, but it was nothing to the painful burning in his chest.

"I would be grateful if you would depart from my forge and my home."

Henry grimaced.

"Henry?"

"Nothing, just...an unpleasant memory," he said quietly.

One day, perhaps, he would share with Peg just what had occurred when he had gone missing. The connection he had shared. The warmth, the love...

Perhaps it would not be a good idea to share that particular sensation.

Henry grimaced as he poured himself another glass of wine. "You are well?"

"You have been *missing*," Peg shot back as she sat beside him on the sofa, eyes narrow. "Just a single letter would have sufficed, you know—that Jenks wouldn't tell me—"

"Good," said Henry heavily. "I instructed him to keep it to himself."

He should have known his sister would not have taken that as sufficient an answer.

"Henry Everleigh," Peg said sternly. "Where have you been?"

It was no use. Henry knew he would have to tell her—at least, tell her something, even if not the whole truth. She deserved to know what he had done to protect her reputation; the lengths he had gone in his hunt to discover who was slandering her.

He looked at her, heart twisting. She was the only family he had left, and he would protect her. Even if he had hoped that one day he and Minny—

A sneeze.

It would not have been remarkable, except that Henry had not sneezed—and he had been looking at Peg in that moment, and neither had she.

She did, however, flush a violent shade of red. "Henry—"

"By God, you've got a man here," Henry breathed, putting down his wine glass and rising to his feet, heart pounding.

"No, I haven't!"

He heard the lie in his sister's anxious voice the moment she spoke. He had thought he'd heard a man's voice when in the hall-way—and that sneeze was certainly not one of the Everleighs.

"Margaret Everleigh, you tell me right this moment," Henry start-ed, raising a finger to point it at his sister.

She leapt to her feet. "You have no right to tell me what I should and shouldn't do, you've gallivanted off with your mistress no doubt for weeks and—"

"I have not—that is beside the point!" Henry blustered.

Oh, how could this have gone so wrong? After everything he'd done to protect Peg's reputation from complete falsehoods, here she was, managing it destroy it all by herself!

"Come out, you blaggard, so I can see you!" Henry shouted.

There was a moment's pause in which his heartbeat throbbed painfully, then...

Then a man, a gentleman from the looks of him, stepped awk-wardly out from behind one of the curtains, a rueful look on his face, his cheeks splotched red.

"Sorry about the sneeze, old thing," he said apologetically.

Fury grasped at Henry's heart and refused to let go. "Sorry!"

"I wasn't actually apologizing to you," said the man stiffly. "To Peg—"

"Don't you dare talk to my sister in that—that tone!" Henry spat, taking a step forward and wondering if it was physically possible to tear a man in half with his bare hands.

Dear God, his sister, alone, with a man! In the house!

If the gossip columns got a hold of this...

Well, that left him with no alternative.

"You, sir, are contemptible," Henry growled. "And after dishonor-ing my sister—"

"Henry!" Peg grabbed at his arm, trying to pull him back.

But Henry was having none of it. After all he had been through, the sacrifices he had made—eating Ted's pies! Sleeping in that godawful bed!—he would not permit a gentleman to spill just how inappropriate the Duke of Dulverton's sister was.

No. Minny had taught him many things, but one of them he would never forget.

Strike while the iron is hot.

"You challenge me, sir?" the man said, his expression darkening.

Henry hesitated. Yes, he did. At least, he would like to march the cur to Hyde Park and shoot him—but duels were hardly appropriate any more, and were severely frowned upon. If they were to be caught...

The whole point was to avoid scandal, wasn't it?

Henry slowly lowered his accusatory finger. "No. No, but I want you gone—from London, from England."

The man's face fell. "Dulverton, you do not know me but I am the Duke of—"

"I don't care if you were Prinny himself, I will not have gentlemen cavorting with my sister!" Henry blustered, feeling heat searing his cheeks. *Oh God, the very thought!*

"Be gone, and be grateful I have no pistol on me at present," Henry said, his chest heaving. "Go on."

For a moment, he was not sure if the man would obey his stricture. Peg was still pulling at his arm, and Henry ignored her as best he could as he stared at the villain before him.

Then the man nodded. "As you wish."

"No—Ashcott, no!"

Henry's heart broke to hear Peg's voice so pained, but it was no good. The man strode out of the room, slamming the door behind him, leaving the Everleigh siblings in silence.

Only then did Henry realize how heavily he was breathing, how his hands were clenched into fists, a red mist descended before his eyes. As he blinked, it started to fade.

Peg's hand slipped from his elbow. "He's...he's gone."

There was agony in her words. Henry saw a tear falling down her cheek. "If he were a man of honor, he would have asked for your hand."

His sister laughed dryly. "Yes. Yes, I suppose he would have done. Perhaps that was why I liked him so much."

Henry's stomach clenched. "You didn't—"

"Henry Everleigh, do not even think to ask me that," Peg said, her cheeks flushing.

She dropped heavily into an armchair.

Mind reeling, hardly able to understand what had occurred, Henry fell in a similar manner onto the sofa where, only minutes before, his sister and that cad of a duke—*if he even was a duke*—had been drinking wine and laughing together.

Had he got this one wrong, too? Was it possible he had leapt into this situation with just as little knowledge as with Minny—and been incorrect again?

"I...Peg, I am sorry," he said awkwardly.

Her dark laugh only increased his sense of guilt. "Don't be. I knew what I was...well. The Duke of Ashcott has a reputation, and not a good one. I was a fool to think I could charm him into...into a commitment of any kind."

Henry nodded as though he understood what had just happened. The world did not appear to wish to stay straight for more than five minutes together.

Minny—her secret—her brother—now Peg?

"You still haven't told me where you have been," Peg said perceptively.

Henry sighed and picked up the glass he had been so swift to abandon. "It's not a topic for a lady, let alone my little sister."

He had not expected his little sister to snort with laughter.

"Little sister? Henry, I am two and twenty years old, more than old enough to hear about your mistress."

Cheeks flaming, Henry protested, "I have not been with my mistress!"

"Well, then?" asked Peg archly. "Where have you been?"

His intention had been to keep the entire thing a secret. Why should Peg have to know just what lengths he had been prepared to go to protect her?

But after the sudden discovery of a man—*a man!*—with his sister, Henry had a rather horrible feeling she was right. She was more than old enough to hear about the underbelly of the world.

More wine disappeared into his mouth. "I have been attempting to discover who has been writing those slanderous lies about you in the newspapers."

Henry was unsure what he had been expecting at those words. Thanks, perhaps? A sense of gratitude? Perhaps embarrassment at the nonsense the newspaper had been printing?

It was therefore gratifying to see pink dots appear once more in his sister's cheeks.

At least Peg would never change—

"What lies?" she asked faintly.

Henry snorted. "Oh, Peggy, you must have seen them! All this nonsense about you sneaking out of Almack's—avoiding Lady Romeril, as though that were possible! The guff about you attending the Old York's. As though any respectable lady would—"

"Ah," said Peg.

Henry blinked. His sister was looking…uncomfortable.

It made no sense. Unless of course, and his spirits rallied, she was affronted at the mere suggestion of such disgraceful rumors. Yes, that must be it. There was no possibility that—

"Is this a bad time to say," his sister said awkwardly, "that…all those stories are true?"

Henry's jaw fell open as horror overcame him. "All are—"

"I mean, I wasn't able to slip past Lady Romeril, that part isn't true, as if anyone could escape her watchful eye," said Peg swiftly, as though these words would in any way mend. "No, I was being chaperoned by the Duchess of Axwick at the time, and I truly felt awful for disobeying her order to stay in Almack's but Ashcott—"

"The blaggard!"

"Henry!"

Henry glared at his sister, hardly able to understand what he was hearing. *All...true?*

All those rumors, lies, slander—not slander at all? Merely an accurate retelling of the mischief his sister was getting up to under his watch?

All sense of what was true and what could be trusted was slipping away. Minny was protecting and supporting those who had no one else to protect them; Peggy was galivanting with gentlemen in the dead of night and frequenting gaming hells of disrepute.

And he...he was in the center. Getting it wrong at every turn.

"You're angry with me, aren't you?" Peg said timidly.

Henry swallowed. It was on the tip of his tongue to say yes, he was absolutely furious. He had trusted her, thought what he was doing was the right thing. Sacrificed his place in Society to go off searching for something that did not exist.

That he had given up soft bedsheets for weeks on this wild goose chase.

But he couldn't. Not with Minny's words ringing in his ears.

"I don't want to hear it. Please leave, Your Grace. I got it right that time, didn't I?"

"I suppose I am," he said hesitantly, unable to lie. "But I am more upset you could not come to me about these things."

Peg laughed dryly as she tucked her feet under her on the chair. "You would have permitted me to go to Vauxhall Gardens unaccompanied?"

Henry's stomach dropped to his knees. "You went—"

"See, I told you," Peg said. "I couldn't come to you, Henry, because you would react so."

"But—but how did it all start?" Henry asked, utterly bewildered.

This was not the Peg he knew—or at least, the Peggy he thought he knew. His little sister was quiet, demure, nervous, shy.

"Well, it did start off with an untrue piece of gossip in the newspapers," Peg admitted. "The most ridiculous thing, a story of me selling off kisses for a shilling—"

Henry's heart twisted painfully, and he tried to prevent himself from interrupting. That had been the first he'd seen, too.

"And then—well, as I was still receiving invitations to the very best parties, I suddenly realized that I was...missing out," confessed Peg with a wry smile. "I mean, if everyone thought I was doing something so scandalous and still considering me excellent company, the question remained, why not enjoy the things I was being accused of?"

Henry went pale. "You didn't sell—"

"Henry Everleigh, the very idea!" His sister looked truly affronted. "No! But I have seen parts of London I was never brave enough to visit, gambled with ruffians and spent...well. Too much time with the Duke of Ashcott, I can see in hindsight. Oh, Henry, I was so bored. And this has been...exciting."

The entire reason he had gone to Pathstow and made Minny's acquaintance in the first place was to end the terrible lies about his sister...lies that were not lies.

Truths about her wild behavior because he was too foolish to see that she was bored.

"I suppose I have acted a little rashly."

Henry barked a laugh. "A little!"

"But don't you see? Everything will be fine, I promise," Peg urged. "Everyone thought the publications false, except Ashcott, naturally, and they will peter out now, won't they?"

"Why?"

His sister laughed again. "Well, I am hardly going to get away with doing such things while you are here, will I?"

Henry's mind had been pulled in so many different directions over the last few days, it was hard to keep track. But of one thing he was absolutely sure.

"You certainly won't," he said firmly. "I suppose we will have to trust this Duke of Ashcoote—"

"Ashcott."

"Whatever—will not reveal the truth of the matter to anyone in the *ton*."

If Henry had been paying attention, he would have seen the look of pain across Peg's face. As it was, he was too busy looking into his empty glass and thinking of Minny to notice.

"I am sure he will never darken my doorway again," said Peg faintly.

Henry heaved a sigh of relief. Well, it may not have ended in the way he had expected—*Lord knows, entirely differently*—but at least he could rest easy now, knowing his sister's name would not be dragged into the headlines again.

"You know, I don't think it's right that ladies should not be able to do all those things," Peg said wistfully. "But—no, do not fear, Henry, I will not fall out with you about it. I said I would cease, and I meant it. This sort of thing is not worth losing friends over, after all."

Pain, swift and sharp, stabbed at Henry's chest.

"Once said, those words can never be unsaid."

"Henry? Henry, you...you did not lose a friend over it, did you?"

It was all Henry could do not to snap at his sister, tell her to mind her own business, tell her that because of her he had made a complete fool of himself.

But as he lifted his eyes, he saw the pain there, the sadness. The regret. The shame, perhaps, and the disappointment that Ashcott's lack of action had burnt into her heart.

And he could say nothing but, "No."

Peg sighed with relief. "Oh, good."

"No, I haven't lost a friend," Henry said bleakly. "I think I have lost the love of my life."

CHAPTER EIGHTEEN

May 13, 1810

W ITH A JOLT to her shoulder and a sense of raucous anger,
Minny smashed the hammer down onto the anvil.

Crash!

The noise echoed around the forge, but she barely heard it. How
many years had she spent in this forge as a child, hearing the hammers
rebounding off the anvil, off metal—if her father grew truly frustrated,
off the walls?

It was as melodious to her ears as music would be to another.

Besides, it was an excellent way to relieve the tension in her bones
and the anger searing through her skull.

Lifting the hammer high over her head, Minny brought it onto the
anvil with all her might again and again and again.

Each time, an image appeared in her mind. Moments in her life she
could have said something, done something, changed the dramatic
way her life had been overturned by a handsome face and winning
words…

"You scoundrel. You miser. You cruel harpy—you villain!"

And she loved him. Oh, she could not deny it, not even to herself,
worse luck. Though she had been suspicious at first—rightly so, as it
turned out—it had been impossible to ignore the charm of his smile,

the way his hands…

Minny gritted her teeth and brought the hammer down once more.

Truly, this was a wonderful way to release one's anger. At least, Minny thought it was being released. Each time the hammer came down, however, the anger within her merely boiled, fuel added to the fire, the heat of her rage coming to a boiling point.

It was so—so unfair!

"You should have said no, Minny Banfield," Minny murmured, the chiming of the hammer on the anvil invading her thoughts but not enough to blot out Henry Everleigh's face.

"No" when he asked to come inside the forge in the first place. "No" when he wanted to learn from her. "No" when he wished to try out the anvil himself. "No" to kisses by the furnace. "No" to…well. All of it.

Minny swallowed. The furnace was not lit, she could not bring herself to actually work today, but was all this rage erupting in ways she could not have predicted? Was it her own bitterness warming the place?

With a heavy sigh, Minny laid aside the hammer. Sparks had flown the last few hits, and as she examined the delicate tool, she could see she had damaged the end.

"The trouble is," she said darkly in the gloomy forge, "is that despite that, despite all the regret, all the pain, all the harm…you miss him."

"Ahem."

Minny whirled round. There was a shadow standing in the doorway, a hand to their mouth as they loudly cleared her throat.

Shame rushed through her. *Of course, the one time she permitted herself to talk aloud about this ridiculous business, there was someone there to overhear her!*

That was it; from now on, unless she was specifically expecting a customer, she was going to keep the forge door locked. It was hard enough to concentrate on smithing when someone wandered in wanting a casual conversation. It was worse still when she wanted to berate herself about falling in love with a brigand, only to have that chastisement overheard!

"Yes?" she snapped.

Her fingers crept to the anvil and picked up the hammer.

Well. One never knew, even in Pathstow. Absolutely anyone could just wander into the place and decide that it was appropriate for them to help themselves to people's doorways.

Just like, Minny thought bitterly, *Mr. Henry Everleigh.*

No, wait, he was a duke, apparently. His highness? His Grace?

"Wood delivery," said the voice.

Minny narrowed her eyes. She was a suspicious soul at heart; her father had always said that—but there was cause to be in this situation.

She was no fool. No matter how much he attempted to hide that voice…

"Henry Everleigh, go away," Minny said wearily, putting the hammer onto the anvil and turning away.

She wouldn't look at him. She couldn't.

Heartbreak had never been something she thought she would suffer. After seeing her brother go through such torment—admittedly, of a different flavor—she had not precisely sworn off men or matrimony. She had thought it would take a great deal for her to be tempted into such foolish longings.

And after only days since she last saw him, Henry was not someone she wished to see.

"Look," Henry's voice behind her said desperately. "I am sure you do not want—"

"You are correct," Minny said to the wall.

"And you are perfectly within your right to—"

"I know," she snapped, turning to glare, wishing to goodness the man did not look so handsome in the fashionable and well-cut jacket he was wearing. His hands were up in surrender. "This is my forge, mine, Henry—Your Worshipfulness, whatever you are, and—"

"That is not up for debate," Henry said, taking another step toward the anvil.

It was instinct that made her do it, and Minny was not particularly proud. Her hand raised, picking up the hammer.

"Stay back," she intoned quietly.

Perhaps it was the softness of her voice that told him just how seriously to take her remark. That, or there was something in her eyes expressing how little patience she had.

Minny hardly knew. She felt as though her hair was standing on end, crackling with the electrifying power of her rage.

How dare he!

Stride back here into Pathstow as though nothing happened—look at her like that, as though she should be grateful he has returned!

As though she was pining for him!

Dreaming about him once—*fine, a few times*—did not count, Minny told herself severely. That was natural, once one had given a man...everything.

She swallowed. She was not going to lose her head. She was not going to give into the temptation to lose her temper and wallop the man, just once, to show him how much he'd injured her.

Minny slowed her breathing, allowed the hackles on the back of her neck to calm, and looked back at Henry.

The idiot still had his hands up. "I just wanted to say—"

"There is nothing you can say to excuse what you have already said," Minny cut across him.

The pain in her heart suggested otherwise. *Traitorous thing!*

She knew she wanted to be convinced. She wanted to forget the argument, the misunderstanding, whatever it was. Leave it behind, to a past that no longer existed.

Wanted to be swept into Henry's arms and kissed...

"Minny, you have to listen to—"

"I don't have to do anything," Minny said brightly, forcing a smile. "And you would be very much mistaken if you think I wish to hear any such speeches from your mouth, Henry Everleigh."

This would have been a remarkably impressive statement, she thought darkly, *if her gaze had not then slipped to the man's mouth.*

Oh, there was a mouth that knew precisely what it wanted—how to give and receive pleasure.

Why, it was here on this very anvil they had...

Minny swallowed and hoped to goodness her cheeks had not been disloyal as the thoughts rushing through her mind. She was not about to be seduced. Again.

There had been a moment, just a moment, when everything could have been right. When striking then, while everything between them was hot and molten and malleable, could have been made into something truly special.

But that moment was gone, wasn't it?

Henry swallowed. Minny tried not to watch the movement of his throat. "I just...let me say my piece, Minny—"

"Miss Banfield."

"—Miss Banfield," he corrected hastily, hands still raised in the air. "Then I will leave you alone. Forever."

Minny hesitated. The idea of never seeing Henry again, of him never appearing at the back door with ax in hand, his smile as they talked, his laughter at her stew when it had burnt most inexplicably at the bottom...

It hurt. It hurt far more than she had expected.

Bother it all!

But she could not allow herself to dream on in ridiculous hope. Hoping that one day he would return to the forge. No, she needed an end to this. A complete break, that was what was needed.

Sometimes iron could not be mended.

"Fine," Minny said, trying to keep bitterness from her voice. She would not let him see how greatly he had injured her. "Speak."

Evidently Henry had not actually believed she would acquiesce. His hands fell to his sides as his eyes widened. "Ah. Ahem. Right."

Minny rolled her eyes. What a pity her heart was so easily swayed.

"Minny, I—Miss Banfield, I mean," Henry added, seeing her flare of irritation. "I just...I was wrong."

Silence followed, during which Minny waited. Surely the man could not imagine those three words were sufficient for assuming the very worst of her!

After what felt like a full minute, it became clear Henry was not going to say anymore.

Despite her better judgment, Minny prodded. "Wrong?"

Henry's shoulders slumped. "So wrong, I do not even know where to start! Oh, Minny, I have never before doubted myself, never before been given any occasion to second guess my opinions or decisions—"

"Lucky you," Minny muttered under her breath.

He grinned awkwardly. "Quite."

Perhaps if he were not so handsome, Minny could not help but think, she would find it easier to throw the brute out. As it was, he looked remarkably fine. The cut of his sleeves gave full accentuation to the muscles he had grown under her care. Muscles that had lifted her bodily onto the—*concentrate, Minny!*

"Being a duke, one never expects to be...well, challenged, to tell the truth," Henry was saying morosely. "One is always right. Servants obey, men fawn, even gentlemen—"

"Sorry, am I meant to be impressed by this, or feel sorry for you?"

He grinned. "I don't know. I suppose I want to explain that being wrong was not something I was raised to be. I was born and bred to be someone in the right, the idea of getting something wrong...no, never."

Minny swallowed. She could see how that could be a problem.

"Until you came here."

"Well, as it turns out, no," Henry said with a frankness she had not expected. "No, the very reason that I came here in the first place, believe it or not, was a great misapprehension."

Now that did not make sense. Minny tried to recall precisely what Henry had said.

"*Because gossip about Lady Margaret Everleigh is lucrative, of course! Because her ruined reputation in the gossip columns of London newspapers undoubtedly sells them, and it is my duty to save that reputation!*"

"Your sister?" she ventured, wondering where all her fire and irritation had gone.

Henry nodded. "The very same. Here I was, gallivanting about the country, lowering myself—sorry—in places like this, all to protect the honor of my sister."

He gave a dry laugh and stepped back, leaning against the bench.

"And you did, didn't you?" she asked, curiosity getting the better of her.

The laugh Henry gave was dark. "No, not entirely. It turns out all the scandalous things being printed in the newspapers, all the outrageous actions, all the disreputable places she was supposedly going to…she was."

He glanced up, finally meeting her gaze with a fierce loyalty for his sister that quite took Minny's breath away.

He was a fine man. Rash, certainly, and bold where he should sometimes be gentle, barreling forward when sometimes he should listen. But he had risked much to protect his sister's honor—and to discover it was her indeed doing the ruining…

"You must have been surprised," Minny managed.

"More or less shocked than finding her drinking with a gentleman in our drawing room near midnight?" Henry mused with a chuckle. "You can imagine."

Minny raised an eyebrow. "Drawing room? No, I cannot possibly imagine."

With a sarcastic curtsey, she gestured around the forge.

Much to her surprise, Henry winced. "You knew what I meant."

It was only then that Minny saw just how much it pained him to admit these actions of his sister. Revealing to her that his entire errand had been only that of a fool's, that the hard work he had put in, the sacrifice of leaving his title behind had all been for nothing...

It aggrieved him. Yet he, in effect, was trusting her with his sister's reputation.

Minny bit her lip. "Yes, I-I know what you meant."

He took a step away from the bench. Minny instinctively took a step away, back touching the wall.

"I am a duke, but that does not mean I am completely immune to fault," Henry said, eyes expressive. "It is only now that I am learning that because my capabilities—no, that is not what I mean, because my privilege is greater, so, too, can be my mistakes."

Minny swallowed. "Mistakes?"

"Like leaving you without fighting for you," he said passionately, his gaze never leaving hers. "Like assuming the worst of you when I knew you already, without knowing of your brother's...of your brother, that you are the best of men. Women. Blast."

A shy smile was threatening to overturn Minny's scowl, though she was doing her best to keep it away. "I knew what you meant."

"Do you? Because I hardly know how to breathe when I am in your presence." Henry's gaze was beseeching, a vulnerability Minny had not seen before. "Believing you should be an instinct, yet I permitted myself to—oh God, the way I spoke to you!"

"You scoundrel. You miser. You cruel harpy—you villain!"

The words rang in Minny's mind, yet the remembrance did not turn her heart away as she had expected.

Now she knew the full story, knew the devotion and loyalty he held for his sister, Henry's words had a different ring to them. As the iron rings differently when it is ready to be molded, to be changed, so

Minny could now hear the change.

He had been pained, hurt, and lashed out.

That was the evidence of his true character. Coming back, apologizing, prostrating himself at her feet?

Well, perhaps not literally, Minny thought, her gaze raking over Henry's face as though seeking a visible truth. *But almost.*

"You spoke from a heart that was broken," she said softly.

Henry laughed as he shook his head. "A heart utterly branded Minny Banfield, which will never be unchanged."

A prickle of delight rushed through her though Minny attempted to push it away. Not forcefully, but still. She would not permit one clever phrase to overtake her heart.

"Very prettily said."

"Very painfully felt," said Henry bleakly.

He took another step forward, and this time Minny had nowhere else to flee…and found she had no wish to.

"Minny—Miss Banfield, sorry—"

"No, I think I like Minny," she breathed.

His smile sparked heat through her chest. "I speak the truth. You are the one who told me about maker's marks. Your maker's mark has been seared into me, and no matter what happens now, even if you never wish to see me again, I cannot unmake myself. I cannot belong to anyone else."

Minny knew herself, knew the danger she was in—but could she truly say her temper had never gotten the better of her? Had she never regretted words spoken in heated anger?

"I really do love you, Minny."

Did she gasp, allow the breath clutched in her lungs to escape? Minny could not tell, but a weight from her shoulders was lifted, and she found she could not lie to herself.

Could not hold back the emotions Henry had awakened in her already.

She breathed quietly, "I don't want to be hurt again."

He winced but took another step forward. Now he was at the anvil. Minny tried not to look at it, the location of such wondrous pleasures she had thought, then, would be something they enjoyed forever.

And then she had lost that certainty. Was Henry here to offer it once more?

"I can't promise I will never make another mistake again—Lord knows, that would be a mistake in itself," Henry said quietly, stepping around the anvil.

Minny knew that if she asked him to stop advancing, if she told him to leave, he would. He would obey her not merely because this was her forge, but because he loved her. Because he respected her too much to hurt her.

But the words did not come. A desperate need for him, not just his kisses but his presence, his laughter, his way of seeing the world, had been stamped down after their disagreement but it could not be ignored forever.

"But I am willing to learn."

"You were a slow learner at the anvil."

Henry grinned. He was now only a few inches away. "I have an excellent teacher."

"And does that mean," Minny said, her heart thumping wildly as she reached forward and stroked the lapel of his impressive woolen coat, "that you will listen and obey me?"

A small groan escaped his lips as he leaned forward, keeping his lips just inches from hers. "I'm an excellent student."

"I think your horse shoes would suggest otherwise," she breathed, intoxicated by his presence. "You'll have to listen closely if you're ever going to make a horse shoe that could actually fit a horse."

Henry groaned, and the words he spoke next were more of a growl than a sentence. "Damnit Minny, don't make me beg."

A mischievous smile crept over her lips as sweet relief swept through her. She had him now, and she would never have to let him go.

Her fingers tightened around his lapel as Minny pulled him forward. "Now that's an idea…"

CHAPTER NINETEEN

May 22, 1810

H ENRY GRINNED. "READY?"
"Absolutely not."

Laughter filled the carriage as it rumbled to a slow halt. Henry had never known such perfect joy—at least, not since leaving the forge.

Now that was a place where he had made some truly spectacular memories, he thought as he leaned back in the sumptuously decorated carriage. He could never look at an anvil in the same way again. Not without feeling a desperate need to place Minny on it and—

"This is rather rebellious of you, though, isn't it?" Minny interrupted his thoughts.

Henry took her hand in his.

"I don't know what you mean," Henry said with a grin.

Not entirely true.

The news that Henry Everleigh, Duke of Dulverton, had returned to London after his mysterious absence with a future bride—one of no family, no fortune, and with callouses on her fingers—had been the absolute talk of the *ton* for several weeks.

Dulverton takes dull wife

Duke presumes society will accept coarse bride

Dulverton name further dragged into the mud

Henry had seen the headlines, despite Peg's attempts to hide them. It was astonishing what one could learn from one's manservant.

"Not that I take any credence of the nonsense, Your Grace," Jenks had added hastily, after sharing the rather lurid headlines.

And Henry had done nothing but laughed.

Reputation? What need he of the newspapers' good wishes?

He was a duke, something no one could take from him. He was a wealthy and—mostly—respected gentleman, something that only his own foolish actions could remove. Thank goodness no one else had been witness to his foolish outburst at the blacksmith's.

And most importantly, he had Minny.

Henry's gaze drifted over the form of his future bride as she sat beside him in the carriage. Every part of her was precious, not just because of her beauty, but because of her strength. It was something he was growing to appreciate, if possible, more with each passing day.

One of those strong fingers dug into his ribs. "You know precisely what I mean, Your Grace," teased Minny, cheeks flushed. "We are not yet married, and you are still taking me to see Dulverton Manor! Does that not strike you as inappropriate?"

Henry shrugged. "Perhaps it is—but as I have no intention of breaking off this engagement, and as I will see you at the altar in just a few weeks, I will just have to hope you do not abscond with my heart before I make you mine."

Minny grinned as she snuggled into him, her head resting on his shoulder. "I am not sure I could be even more yours than I am already."

Warmth spread across Henry's heart.

She was right. They had attempted not to indulge in lovemaking, but it had been difficult. Even Ted at the King's Head had raised an eyebrow at his late returns when the inn was about to be closed up for the night.

The carriage continued to slow, and Henry glanced out of the window. The familiar avenue of beeches met his eyes and something of the tension around his shoulders melted away.

There was nothing like coming home.

"Here we are," he murmured.

Minny lifted her head from his shoulder to look, and a great deal of satisfaction poured through him as he watched her eyes widen.

"Goodness, you have some very impressive neighbors."

Henry blinked. "I beg your pardon?"

"Well, look at this place!" Minny said, pointing at the window and the magnificent castle they could make out through the trees. "Several stories high, turrets, I am sure there is a dungeon in there somewhere! What is the owner like?"

"Oh, an absolute scoundrel."

"I can see that just from his battlements," Minny nodded approvingly. "Terrible with women, I suppose."

"Truly awful," Henry said truthfully.

"And a scoundrel, you say? We shall to make sure we avoid—why are you smiling?"

Henry quickly forced his face to be serious. "I'm not smiling."

"Yes, you are," Minny said accusingly. "Why?"

"Because," said Henry quietly as the carriage turned to meander down the drive toward the magnificent castle, "I am that scoundrel."

For a moment, she simply stared, utterly astonished, as Henry's heart beat painfully in his chest. *Had he mistaken the growing rapport between them—had he accidentally—*

Minny's snort echoed around the whole carriage. "Henry Everleigh, you devil!"

"Guilty as charged," he said happily, squeezing his beloved's hand as the carriage drew up outside the castle.

"But you—you never said that—"

"It would be most uncouth for a gentleman to boast about the size of one's…castle," said Henry with mock severity.

Minny's eyes were wide. "But you said—you said it was called Dulverton Manor!"

"And so it is," Henry said briskly, opening the door before the driver or footmen could reach it, and stepping out into the fresh morning air. "Dulverton Manor. Was this not what you excepted?"

Such joy overwhelmed him as his future bride stepped out of the carriage—without a helping hand, naturally—and stared at the impressive façade that was the welcoming East Side of the castle.

This was his home. And yet somehow, it had never felt complete.

Perhaps that was why it was so relatively easy for him to disappear into Pathstow and assume the life of a mere man, leaving behind the duchy and all it entailed.

Only now that Minny was standing before him in the spring sunshine did Henry see just what he had been missing. A wife. A companion, a partner—a truly better self.

"Welcome to your new home," he said softly.

Minny's gaze flickered between his face and the castle. "If this is a trick, Henry—"

"Would I dare to risk your wrath?" Henry said bracingly, pulling her hand into his arm and striding forward. "Come on, let me take you on the tour."

It was not so much a tour as a swift walk. Once, when Henry had been young, he and Peg had surreptitiously followed the housekeeper of the time around the place when she was giving a tour to a few people who had come up from London.

There was so much of Dulverton Manor, that was the trouble. One could simply not take in the place in one visit. Two dining rooms, three drawing rooms, library, study, morning room, orangery, billiards room, smoking room, gun room…and that was just one floor.

"You seriously cannot tell me that this wing is your sister's? The whole wing?"

Henry shrugged as they reached the top of the second staircase, sunlight drifting lazily through the oriel windows along the corridor. "Why not?"

"Because...because..." spluttered Minny, her eyes wide as they stepped into Peg's drawing room. The place was lavishly furnished, as only the sister of a duke would expect. "An entire wing?"

"Well, it was designed as the Dower Wing, but as our mother has sadly died, I thought it was only right that Peg—Margaret had a place of her own," Henry explained with a laugh. "Which may, in hindsight, have precipitated her lack of inhibitions when she went to town."

"Too accustomed to getting her own way?"

Henry grinned as he saw Minny's raised eyebrow. "Something like that."

"I like her already."

His heart twisted with joy and more than a little relief. Now he was starting to get to know Peg all over again, he had been astonished to find she was perhaps just as strong-willed as his future wife.

"Come, I want to show you something," he said impetuously.

Minny laughed as he pulled her faster back to the main staircase and up again. "Really? You have shown me so little up until now!"

His heart soared as he opened the door Henry knew he absolutely should.

His bedchamber.

"Oh, my..." Minny breathed, head tilting up.

It was what everyone did the first time they stepped into the ducal bedchamber.

At least, Henry thought wretchedly, *no one* else *ever would.* This was Minny's domain now. All past mistakes were—hopefully—behind him. Now there'd be only fresh ones.

"This place is truly stupendous," Minny whispered under the impressive painting.

Henry nodded. He had thought that, the first time he had been

201

ushered into the place. Some said it was definitely a Michelangelo—if anyone could prove he had been to England. Others said it was a da Vinci, though how they explained that as the man had never even left Italy, Henry did not know.

"Whoever had painted it was clearly a master," he said aloud.

Minny squeezed his arm without looking away from the painting. "Or a mistress."

Dear God, he would never stop being challenged by this woman, would he? And, Henry found with delight he had no wish to.

Minny Banfield was a treasure, not because she could be beaten into submission like a piece of iron to fit the role of duchess that Society expected of her.

No. Henry would keep her just as she was—much like the rest of his horse shoe attempts. It really was a tricky piece of work, he had tried to tell Minny only yesterday, and it was shameful that she took such delight in teasing him about his efforts.

"Well, this will be our bedchamber," he said aloud.

Pink tinged Minny's cheeks as she slipped her hand from his arm. "Truly?"

Henry nodded. "Just a few weeks…"

It was impossible to keep the longing from his voice, but he had no need to censure himself before Minny. She knew his desires, shared in many of them. Had already shared some of them. And there was so much more to enjoy…

Henry shivered.

"Cold?"

"With you? Never," he said with a laugh. "But I suppose you will have to accustom yourself to living a life of wealth and splendor now. It's quite a come down for a woman I considered a harpy."

Minny punched him, gently, though with far more force than a lady would, on the arm. "You and your nonsense, Henry."

"I think you will find that it's your nonsense, actually—ouch!"

"Serves you right," Minny said nonchalantly.

Henry staggered backward, clutching at his arm in mock agony. "I am wounded!"

"Only because I am stronger than you."

The witty retort could not have come from more delectable lips. A rush of desire in his loins followed as Minny walked to the window and looked out at the gardens.

What was he going to do with himself whenever she was in his presence? He became an absolute fool—Peg had already said how the very mention of Minny was enough to make him tongue-tied.

Thankfully he would have the rest of his life to grow accustomed to it.

"What a spectacular garden," Minny said softly.

Henry swelled with pride. It was rather spectacular, if he said so himself.

Though now he came to think about it, it was foolish of him to take such pride in it. It had been his great-grandfather who had landscaped, his grandfather who had planted the trees, and his father had planted the borders.

Well. Their servants.

"I do like it," he said aloud. "The lawn in summer is particularly useful for cricket and other such pursuits. And there's the park, of course."

"Park?"

"Woodland and open grassland, where the deer live."

Immediately Henry knew he had said something rather ridiculous, for Minny turned and grinned. "Deer?"

"Well, a gentleman has to have some sport," he said defensively.

Minny giggled. "Yes, I can see it would be dreadfully dull living here otherwise."

"I don't know what you—Minny Banfield! Are you cheeking me!"

She turned, leaning against the window with laughter dancing in her eyes. "Absolutely."

Henry's heart soared. What had he done to deserve such happiness, such perfect completion in the arms of another?

"No vegetables, though." Minny gestured to the window. "Very pretty flowers, I am sure, but no vegetables. Now, in my opinion, a garden should have vegetables."

It was all Henry could do not to smile. "That's why I have kitchen gardens. So everything you see here is on the west side of the house, but the entirely of the south gardens are kitchen gardens. Apples, pears, carrots, potatoes, leeks—"

Minny laughed with a wry shake of her head. "I suppose I should have expected that. South side of the house, west side of the house…"

She continued to shake her head as she turned back to the window.

Henry's happiness was momentarily tempered. It was a huge change, he knew. Even before he had returned to fight for her, iron out the mistakes he had made, he had known.

If Minny wished to be a part of his life, it would be here. Not at the forge, the place where she felt most powerful, most at home. No, the Duchess of Dulverton would live here, beside him. A great change for a woman who had always worked for a living.

Was he asking too much of her? Was he demanding such a relinquishment of everything she was that eventually Minny would look around and see not beauty and elegance, but a cage?

Henry swallowed. His voice was serious as he asked, "Do you think you can be happy here?"

When Minny did not immediately respond, continuing to look out across the carefully manicured lawns, his stomach lurched painfully, and all the panic that had swept through him at the thought of losing her the first time reared its ugly head.

He could not live without her—but he was no cad, to force her into a life that could not make her happy. Was he about to lose the only woman he now knew he could love? He could not be without her, he—

There was a wicked smile on Minny's face. "There's a village we passed a mile back."

Henry nodded. It was not precisely the response he had been expecting, but—

"Do they have a smithy?"

What an odd question. "No. Actually, there was talk about a year ago about building one in the hope someone would come and...oh, no. No, Minny, absolutely not!"

Henry groaned as Minny giggled and took his hands in hers.

"It was just an idea! A little smithy, just a mile away, hardly a long walk—"

"You cannot be serious!"

Minny's eyes twinkled with mischief. "I don't want to lose who I am, and if your village needs a blacksmith..."

Henry sighed, though he knew immediately he would be unable to say no. Not that it would matter. Minny Banfield did what she liked, and he saw no way of stopping her.

Besides, she would be the Duchess of Dulverton. It was hard to say no to a duchess.

"You really are going to test me, aren't you?" he said amiably.

Minny raised an eyebrow. "Quickest way to test a metal is to place him in the fire."

Henry groaned. "Yes, I can see that."

His heart fluttered with all the exciting possibilities. Minny, in a forge of her own a mile from their home. Returning with soot across her hands. Helping her to slowly remove those working clothes—

"But what about your forge?" Henry said, his concentration returning to the matter at hand rather than the delightful imaginary images cascading through his mind. "It was your family forge, you cannot simply give it up."

Minny sighed. "What am I supposed to do, transport it here?"

"It's not the worst idea."

Her astonished look made Henry laugh as he shook his head. *She had a great deal to learn about what money could do.*

"You think you could—what, transport it brick by brick almost fifty miles?" Minny's eyes were wide with astonishment.

Henry shrugged. "I suppose it would be possible—if that is what you would like."

He held his breath as he watched Minny consider. There was something about that forge; it was precious to him, yes, but was a talisman of the life Minny was leaving behind. A proof of the danger she had put herself in, sending messages for her brother and his network.

A reminder he had not always been in her life.

Henry tried to push the thought away. He was no brute, to force his wife to abandon everything she was merely because she was now married! Still, it would be a perpetual reminder if it were to be moved to Dulverton village…

"No," said Minny decidedly.

Henry sagged with relief. "Good."

"No, I think I will give it to a friend of mine," Minny said, squeezing Henry's hands. "Two friends of mine, actually. A pair of ladies, they have been looking for a way to make a living for themselves, and the work there will not be so arduous with two."

There was something in the way she spoke that made Henry wonder. Two ladies…two ladies living together, in need of an occupation. If anyone else had said those words, he would likely as not have given them no heed whatsoever. As it was…

"These ladies," Henry said awkwardly. "They are…friends?"

Minny grinned. "Friends of mine."

Well, if there was ever anyone better suited to carry out the work that Minny had been doing there—both in the forge, and for the network of those who loved so differently from what he had imagined—a pair of ladies may be the perfect fit.

"I suppose I should expect nothing less than you installing the right people into the place," he said aloud.

"Quite right, too," said Minny firmly. "Now, there is one thing in this room I simply do not understand and demand an explanation to."

This was not what he had expected. Henry nodded, eager to help, eager to make his home as welcome to her as the forge had been to him. Though arguably, a little less dirty.

"Of course—what is it?"

Not taking her eyes from him, Minny pulled Henry toward the capacious bed, covered in silk coverlets, and raised an inquisitive eyebrow. "What on earth is this for?"

Henry chuckled as he pulled her into his arms and started trialing burning kisses down Minny's neck. "Oh, 'tis a most complicated piece of equipment. Here, let me show you..."

EPILOGUE

June 5, 1810

"READY?" MINNY'S VOICE almost vibrated with excitement. It had taken a great deal of planning to get here—planning and intrigue.

But when one had friends all over the country in a large network dedicated to love, it was not impossible to organize what felt like the impossible.

Still. She was rather surprised Henry had been willing to wear the blindfold for the last hour or so.

"Ready for what?" came Henry's voice with confusion.

Minny rolled her eyes, excitement propelling her forward with a fizz in her chest.

"Ready to descend the carriage, of course," she said, brushing back a curl of hair threatening to drop over her eyes. "Here, take my hands."

It had been difficult to persuade Henry to come with her on a mysterious journey of two days. *At least,* Minny corrected, *it had been easy to persuade Henry.* It had been difficult to persuade the Duke of Dulverton.

"A duke," he had told her only three days ago, "has responsibilities!"

"Yes," Minny had reminded him. "And some of those responsibilities are to me…"

It was a relief, really, he had agreed to come with her. So much planning had gone into the whole thing, Minny was not sure she could ever face her brother if the whole thing had been called off.

"Careful," she said as she gently guided Henry down from the carriage.

He snorted. "How on earth can I be careful with you placing this blindfold on my face—and by the way, I think it most outrageous thing that you have done so!"

"I am sure you do," Minny said cheerfully, helping him to step blindly forward.

There, that should do. He would have the perfect view when she finally removed the blindfold.

Exhilaration poured through her chest. When he saw what she had done…

"Our wedding is in just a week, you know," said Henry, turning his head this way and that as though that would help him see. "We have much to do, much to prepare—the last thing we need is an excuse to gallivant about the place! Where are we, anyway?"

Minny tried to keep the anticipation from her voice as she released his hands. "Our wedding isn't in a week."

Even under the blindfold, she could see a look of panic rush across her future husband's face. "It—it isn't? Minny, if I have offended you by something I have said or done, you must tell me so I can apol—"

"Our wedding," Minny said softly, tugging apart the knot of his blindfold, "is today."

She held her breath and tangled the cotton blindfold in her fingers as Henry blinked in the early morning air.

His eyes focused on what was before them. "Oh, no!"

"Oh, yes," said Minny happily.

"No!"

"Absolutely."

Henry turned his gaze wildly to her. "You haven't—"

"I absolutely have," Minny said with a laugh, joy swooping in her stomach.

He groaned, though a smile was already appearing. "You shouldn't have."

"Perhaps not," she admitted, though now she had seen his reaction, it was impossible to regret her choice. "But there we are."

"But my sister—the church! Lord, all the invitations have been sent, even Lady Romeril has deigned to—"

"All the more reason," said Minny, leaning against the village sign that carefully spelt *Gretna Green*, "to marry here."

Henry laughed as she embraced him, pouring into the connection all the eagerness she had forced herself to keep silent on their journey.

It was perfect; she was certain he would see that. *Once he got used to the idea*, Minny thought impishly. He would see just how perfect it was.

"I don't know why I am so surprised," Henry said ruefully, still shaking his head. "I should have guessed something was up when you paid little heed to your bridal gown fitting."

Minny made a face. "All that lace!"

"It is expected of a duchess, you know," he reminded her.

The sound of the word caused a lurch in her chest Minny could not ignore. *Duchess*. Yes, she would become a duchess in just a few minutes. But that did not mean she had to act like a duchess before that, did she?

She was a blacksmith. If there was ever a day to *be* a blacksmith, it was her wedding day.

"You are truly not angry?" Minny asked.

Henry kissed her forehead as his hands slipped to her buttocks. "How could I ever be angry at you?"

"Quite easily, as it turns out."

"Oh, hush," he said good naturedly, striding forward with Minny beside him, his arm still around her. "This is…well, certainly not what I had expected…"

Minny grinned as they walked through the small, sleepy village in the direction of the gentle hammering which grew louder with every step. "Good."

Perhaps she should have spoken about it with him beforehand. He might have agreed with her—that the frivolities of a ducal wedding were starting to get far more ridiculous than even she had dreamed.

Oh, a simple wedding, where one walked to church—or as it happened, the anvil—on a bright summer day, with her future husband's arm around her…

That was all Minny had wanted. When she had thought about it at all, of course. She'd had more than enough time to think about it in the last few weeks, and with Peg's help, she had managed it.

She was going to be a handful, that sister-in-law of hers.

"I hope you're proud of yourself." Henry's words brought her from her reverie.

Minny grinned as they turned a corner and saw the smithy. "Very."

He laughed. "You know, you never cease to amaze me."

"Good! I was starting to worry that I would have nothing to teach you," she admitted as they reached the forge door.

And for some reason, Henry halted there. "Truly?"

Minny swallowed. She was still growing accustomed to revealing her vulnerabilities, her insecurities. A woman living on her own, even in a respectable village like Pathstow, could not broadcast her concerns too widely.

Strength and fire. That was what she had clung to.

For too long. Now it was time, as she looked into the loving eyes of Henry Everleigh, Duke of Dulverton, to melt.

"Truly," she admitted. "I like the idea of teaching you, of having some sort of wisdom or knowledge that you don't."

Henry nodded. "Well, I think you're safe there."

Minny frowned. "I am?"

"Not only will I never be able to perfect the horse shoe—I don't know what it is, I seem to have a block about the damned thing," he said with a smile, "but I have another teacher now."

It was such an unexpected statement for her beloved to make that Minny found herself stepping away. "I beg your pardon?"

"Not like that!" Henry said hastily, raising his hands in the all too familiar sign of surrender. "No, I just meant—I have taken up fencing! Again, I suppose, I was taught as a boy but I was truly terrible, even Peg was better than—I have a friend, a duke actually, who is teaching fencing. Will be, at least, when he returns to London. Whenever that is."

Minny hesitated, trying to take in the rush of words. "A duke teaching fencing?"

Henry sighed, and a shadow crept over his face. "He had a terrible time in the war. Oh, what he saw there...anyway, he is in Oxford at the moment recovering and then will return to London, I am sure. I thought, while we try to keep Peg under control—"

"Easier said than done."

"—I thought I would take up fencing again," Henry finished. "Do not fear, you have no true competition—unless you are about to reveal you can fence as well as you can forge."

Minny laughed, all joy restored. She had been foolish to think Henry—no, he was loyal to a fault, was this man. If his sister could put him through such a painful time, she was likely to have Henry's loyalty for the rest of her life.

"You were jealous."

"I was not," she said instinctively. "Well. Maybe. But I will admit, I will not be able to teach you to fight with swords. Though I can teach you to make them."

Henry's eyes widened. "What?"

Minny nudged him. "Look at you, with your uncouth ways!"

"I mean, I beg your pardon!" he corrected with a slight red appearing in his cheeks. "You can make swords?"

Sometimes he would astonish her. But sometimes...

"I am a blacksmith, aren't I?" she pointed out. "Now, there is one more thing before we go in there."

A villager walked past them, a knowing look on her eyes as she glanced at them.

Henry shook his head as she turned a corner. "The arrogance of the woman! Why, she assumes we are here because we have been careless and got you with child!"

Minny cleared her throat.

"Little does she know that we *love* each other," he continued staunchly. "We would not be so thoughtless as to fall with a child before we were wed."

A strange sort of tingling was spreading up Minny's spine, rising slowly with every foolish word her wonderful duke was saying. Oh, she could not have dreamt of a better moment! Gifted to her perfectly, this was the time to—

"As if we would be so foolish!" Henry said with a hearty sniff. "After all, I—what? Why are you looking at me like that?"

Minny had tried her best to hide her smile, but it was almost impossible with him going on like that, speaking such nonsense.

"Oh, nothing," she said airily, watching his face closely for every reaction. "It's just that I am with child. That's all."

It was perhaps a good thing they were standing so close to the smithy, for at her words, Henry reached out a hand and clutched the wall.

"No," he breathed.

Minny swallowed. Henry's face was pale, his eyes wide, and his mouth gaping like a fish. Had she struck too soon? Ought she have waited until they were actually married before revealing such—

"Oh, Minny!"

And then she had no breath to think. Henry had pulled her into his arms and kissed her fiercely on the mouth, his hands clutching her as though she was the most precious gold.

Sizzles of delight rushed through her, and Minny gave herself entirely to the kiss, clinging to the man she loved.

Eventually, she knew not how, she managed to release herself. "You are not angry?"

"Angry?" repeated Henry, his eyes wild. "That there'll be a little one of you and a little one of me out in the world by the year's end?"

"Forged in fire," she said wryly.

"And more welcome than any forge, I can tell you that," he said with a laugh. "Is this why you rushed me up here?"

"Well, partly," Minny conceded. "A week will make all the difference to explaining why this little one has come 'early,' after all."

Wild excitement was clearly still rushing through Henry's mind, and she watched, basking in the way he was taking in the news.

A baby. A family, forged perhaps in a stranger way than most. A proof of their passion for each other, and a child who could be raised in a world, Minny hoped, where love of all kinds was cherished and valued.

Henry pulled a hand through his hair. "I suppose I should make an honest woman of you!"

"If you don't mind," said another voice with a tinge of mockery. "I wish that you would! Come on, stop clogging up my door."

Minny whirled around to see the blacksmith standing in the doorway—a door that had opened, apparently without either of them hearing it.

Heat flushed her cheeks, though that could be the heat pouring through from the forge. Her heart softened. How could she be uncertain in a forge?

"After you, my lady," Henry bowed, extending his hand.

Minny could not help but smile as she stepped into the forge. There was something so comforting about a place like this, so like her own—though there were a few differences.

"How fascinating," she said, stepping away from Henry who had followed her, and toward the rack of tools. "You use several—"

"Minny," Henry said. "We are here to get married, not compare notes on anvils."

Guilt twisted her heart as she turned round to see the blacksmith raise a curious eye. "Yes. Yes, of course—though afterward, perhaps, you could tell me—"

"Minny Banfield, come here and marry me at once!" said Henry, frowning with that imperious command that she had spotted when she had first met him.

And her insides melted. How could she think of anything when Henry was here? The man she loved, craved, that she would argue with and make up with all the days of her life?

Giving no thought to how it may look, Minny strode across the forge, met Henry in the middle, and kissed him impetuously at the anvil.

"Nice anvil," she said without taking her gaze from him. "I'm having mine transported to Dulverton."

"Not going to leave it behind for your...friends?"

Minny's smile became mischievous as the blacksmith took their hands and placed them together. Henry's calluses were starting to fade already, but the impact their time together in the forge would never cool.

"Certainly not," Minny said, hoping he could see precisely what she was thinking by the sparkle of her eyes. "Not after what you and I shared on that anvil."

And she reveled in the way he groaned, unable to say anything in response as the blacksmith began the speech that would make them husband and wife.

About Emily E K Murdoch

If you love falling in love, then you've come to the right place.

I am a historian and writer and have a varied career to date: from examining medieval manuscripts to designing museum exhibitions, to working as a researcher for the BBC to working for the National Trust.

My books range from England 1050 to Texas 1848, and I can't wait for you to fall in love with my heroes and heroines!

Follow me on twitter and instagram @emilyekmurdoch, find me on facebook at facebook.com/theemilyekmurdoch, and read my blog at www.emilyekmurdoch.com.

Made in the USA
Columbia, SC
07 April 2023

14430999R10122